# Stranger's Love: Family's Blood

To Ms Small

Tahmina

with Love

x x x

# Stranger's Love: Family's Blood

*'The faith of a stranger takes you a long way.'*

Based on a true story

Farishta and Tahmina Farhang

| Library of Congress Control Number: | | 2010911987 |
|---|---|---|
| ISBN: | Hardcover | 978-1-4535-5837-9 |
| | Softcover | 978-1-4535-5836-2 |
| | Ebook | 978-1-4535-5838-6 |



This book was printed in the United States of America.

**To order additional copies of this book, contact:**
Xlibris Corporation
0-800-644-6988
www.xlibrispublishing.co.uk
Orders@xlibrispublishing.co.uk
300665

I Farishta dedicate this book to someone very special that without them this book would have no existence. And if that person is reading this . . .just two very small words, that have a great meaning . . . Thank you.

I Tahmina dedicate this book to my wonderful teachers at Lode Heath School who showed me that I have something very special in me and that all I needed was to search for it. And I did. Mr Slattery and Mrs Daniels thank you for believing in me.

We both sincerely dedicate this book to our father; our voice of reason, our courage and our belief. Without him believing in us there would be no book today. Thank you daddy.

To our mother, our family and friends thank you for the support.

Finally, a little phrase which may take you a long way, dedicated to all of our readers: "No matter how many doors shut in your face or how harsh life gets, just remember, where there is courage there is hope."

# Contents

# Chapter 1

## Me, Myself, and I

'Please, just listen to me. I haven't done anything. You're taking it the wrong way. Please, Mum . . . Dad, you have to believe me.' Warm tears fell from my eyes as my hand gripped onto my Hello Kitty bag.

'Get out, Angel! I'm ashamed to even have named you as an angel. You bring disgrace to the name itself. I named you Angel because angels are meant to be clean—clean from heart and soul but, today, you proved me wrong, very wrong, and you put shame to the name and to my legacy! Get out my house!'

My dad's voice was like a jab in the ribs. My heartbeat was fast . . . then it got faster, and then at its fastest point. I could feel warm blood shooting through my veins. From where I was standing, it looked like a horror movie set—closed up and quiet—too quiet. I looked up to the grey-and-white ceiling of the kitchen, and I asked myself, 'Why God, oh, why God?'

The room suddenly blackened out as I found myself back at my university accommodation. Sometimes, the recollection is so clear that I can remember the itch of the suitcase under my hands. OK, whoa! Stop right here. Now I presume you're wondering what I'm doing at my university accommodation when

I should be home just like you—home with family or maybe you're thinking what actually went on that day, that argument, right?

Well . . . of all of the facts of my life, this is the one that wouldn't change. If I ever had the chance to change the past, that shaped hole in my heart, I would!

My name is Angel. I am twenty, and this is my tragedy—a tragedy that will bring tears to your heart and sympathy to your blood. I'm Angel Khan, and this is my tragedy—a journey through fire and blood and what happens when a stranger walks through the path of my life and everything seems to be OK. But before I even begin my tragedy, you should probably know some main facts about me. Here's the description of myself, summarised in just a few words:

Angel Khan
Twenty years of age
Lives in London
Status: Single
Likes: Indian movies (action, comedy, and horror)
Dislikes: *Love* (anything to do with it)
***Regrets: Her Past!***

There you go. Do you know me yet? OK, overlook everything else, and just look at the one in bold writing: ***Regrets: Her Past!*** Yep, if I could take time back and start my memory clean, start my early years again, and re-build my dreams, I would do anything just to take back the hands of time. But I can't . . . I guess that's what hurts the most. Life wasn't as easy as I had imagined; it wasn't full of happiness and joy.

'*Your life is never a straight motorway, it's full of roundabouts,*' my grandmother would always draft at me. Or my grandfather would declare to me my all-time favourite quote, '*It's destiny my child,*' but I was by no means sure about any of the things that they had thrown at me, especially 'destiny.' I'm not sure if I believe in destiny; to be honest, I just think the actions we take today are the consequences we face tomorrow, and we just simply name that destiny. What do you think? In a way, I don't understand how my life really worked out like this; I had never planned it, but maybe, God had. The actions we play today do actually play a big part in our future someday, and that's how I'm trying to learn from my actions of the past; yet my father once told me that now it's too late—running back through fire when there's nothing left to save. It's like running after the very last train when you know it's too late to catch. You see, surely this isn't right. Surely we can change and learn from the mistakes of our past or can we? Nevertheless, one thing I have discovered in my lifetime and that is: whatever mistake we do, there's just simply no erasing it; we can only learn from it. My teacher once said, 'Your future lies before you like a sheet of driven snow. Be careful how you tread, for every step will show.' Just like mine did!

I come from an Asian background—a Westernised culture. My parents were not always that strict, and neither were they strict Muslims, but yet the only rule was the most important rule, and it was the none-boyfriend rule! *Boys not allowed. Full stop.* This rule was in accordance with our religion and our culture. In my language, it's a big *Gunah*, which means sin; therefore, you can understand why we are not allowed a boyfriend—as it goes against everything we believe in Islam. Like I mentioned, just remember that my childhood is very diverse to many other teenagers. For an Asian mother, her biggest fear concerning her daughter would be for her to have a boyfriend at a young age. Conversely for boys, this concern is not such a big compact as it is for girls. It is *haram* (dirty) for an Asian Muslim girl to lose her virginity before marriage. It was a big offence then and till today in the twenty-first century. It's a big offence now, and for that reason, you can understand again why we are not allowed a boyfriend. The truth is that children are conceived for less than admirable reasons these days, especially Asian kids—to glue a bad marriage together, to keep the family name alive, and to mould in their parents' own image!

Well, my outlook to this . . . yeah, I agree with it in some parts than others, and I do accept that young girls should not lose their virginity at such a young age. They should wait for the right one, but, of course, at an appropriate age. Yet we Westernised girls have been brought up in a different society, and we are bound to do things that go against our will, culture, and even sometimes our religion—our bodies seek for pleasure, while our heart seeks for love.

# Chapter 2

## Amar/Best Friend/School

On the subject of boys—I have a best friend named Amar. Well . . . what can I say about him? He is one of a kind. He has been with me ever since I can remember—a best friend and a brother. Amar and I have been through thick and thin, dark tunnels, rainy days, and through sadness and happiness. He's just about four months older than me, and we had met by the bus stop near my house. It was my first day back at George Hill School after the year of my elder brother's death. I remember the exact time and date: 14 April 2006, 9.05 a.m. Isn't it amazing how we remember dates like these, while we forget our mothers' birthdays? How a best friend might seem more important to you than the blood of a family member! Strange, isn't it?

That very mid-April morning, there he was standing by the bus stop. I had never really seen him around before or, maybe, I had but just hadn't noticed his imperfection. Anyway, there he was, leaning on the bus stop window, hard like a tree onto its trunk. Amar was wearing a red Nike jacket and, of course, the school uniform. I just stared at him looking blank.

'Is there something in my teeth?' he alleged.

'Ummm . . . no sorry,' I frowned back. 'You got the time,' I quickly added.

'Yeah, sure, it's 9.15 a.m.' He took his phone out and replied to me in a very surprisingly well-mannered way.

'Thanks.' I smiled at him.

The 220 Bus came, and we both hopped on to it. It was packed. We were late for school too. I remember that in April it had poured down with rain—a lot! Just my bad luck! I was wearing my new dolly shoes—I guess my style really didn't go with the season. My school books were extremely heavy; I had carried too many books than I had needed that day. Actually, I do that all the time—carry extra books and folders than I actually need. Stupid habit—to be honest! Right?

From the corner of my hazel green eyes, I could see a quick glare from Amar, but I didn't exactly figure out what he was trying to say. Then I caught his brown eyes staring back at me. The beats of my heart got fast . . . faster than at its fastest point—like a drum getting louder and louder. For a split second, I thought I heard my heartbeat, even though I could barely hear myself think from all the noises around me. Suddenly, Amar mouthed something at me. I looked behind just to make sure that he was talking to me, and then looked back at him. Still I couldn't understand his sign language. Then from the pushing and shoving of the crowd, I figured he was pointing at me to come towards him. I pushed past through the stampede of people who were surrounded around me; it was like a prison barrier around me. Luckily, Amar's hand grabbed me and pulled me towards him. The staring of the crowd got even horrendous at me, and I could feel the bad force of energy shooting towards me.

'Wow, they're really not going to like you after today, are they?' he joked with me.

'Nope, I guess.' I tried to sound cute, but just didn't work as I'm not the flirty type. He held my hand. 'Let's go to the top bunk, it's where I belong,' he said as he winked at me. Before I could even say OK, I found myself on the top bunk, back seats. Then he started to make conversation with me to pass time, of course, and to get to know a girl like me. No, I am kidding; he was just making conversation!

'My name is Amar, sixteen, got a girlfriend but need a best friend.' He gave me another cute wink and started to joke again. But jokes never worked for me—I mean I just don't get them. I pushed out a laugh not to look rude.

'My name is Angel, fifteen, no boyfriend and need a best friend too.'

'Wow! Already we got something in common.'

'Yeah, we sound like "Dick and Dom."' Oh my god! What was I thinking, 'Dick and Dom!'? How lame could I possibly get? No really, would you ever say this to a cute, friendly sixteen-year-old who is trying to make friends with you?

'You're not so good with jokes, are you?'

Then even before I could answer him, he quickly said, 'Don't worry, I'm not either.' Then for the rest of the drive to school, we just talked about many random things.

Twenty minutes later, I found myself at the top of the school gates. From the distance that I and Amar were standing, I could see the big school building—'George Hill School.' Just below the school name, Mr Marshall—1993 was carved, and I assumed that he was the head teacher of the school.

'Welcome to my other world,' Amar said excitedly, almost to a point where I could feel his excitement. 'I call it a second world, because I am so free and different here. Trust me, Angel, I have been through so many dark tunnels in my life that when I'm in my own house, I'm so closed up, and I feel almost like a prisoner. No one will ever really understand my life.'

'I understand, trust me. I truly do. I tried, I tried, and am still trying, but now in the inside, I feel like I'm dying. That's how hard I try to put a fake smile out for this world. Every day I go through a different phase of time, different dark hours, and different pains,' I finished off with a sad smile.

Amar came up to me and gave me hug. 'We really do have a lot in common, ey? My grandmother was right then, huh, *"Life without friends is like death without witnesses."*'

'I understand.' I gave him a warm smile.

I entered the school hall, and stillness fell across the whole room. The atmosphere of the hall was so cold; it felt like a thunderstorm had just hit the roof of the school. My whole body felt stiff as a stick.

'Miss Sexy is back.' A deep voice came from the background.

'Whoop, whoop.' Another voice came.

'Oh my god! My main girl, Angel.' A very soft voice came from behind me.

My eyes were searching round real quick to see who had said that, and I could sense the tensed atmosphere. All the glaring of the students made me feel tongue-tied.

'Looks like they already know you, ey, Angel.' Amar came and cleared the tense atmosphere.

'Ummm . . . yeah, I used to come to this school one year ago.'

'Well, now it makes sense, because everyone was talking about you before you were even here,' Amar told.

Meanwhile, a sudden mumbling had gone on between everyone. Obviously, I could figure out it was about me. It was like a zoo of animals. Countless of students came to me and started introducing themselves again and asking the common question, 'Do you remember me, Angel?' And I couldn't be rude and say no, so I just said, 'Oh yeah, nice to see you again,' even though, I had no idea who half the dozen of those people were, I mean, how could I remember them when I was going through that sad phase of time when my whole world had fallen apart?

A very pretty blonde with bright blue eyes and hair like 'Rapunzel's' entered, who I don't think I remember, but figured it could be Amar's girlfriend as she gave me a very warm smile. At that time, two minutes later, I found her next to me.

'Hey, babes! You're Angel, right?'

'Yeah, Amy, right?'

'I love your name, Angel. It's so unique and nice.' She smiled at me.

'Thanks, Amy. Well, you know my Asian parents, they say I'm an Angel, but I wish sometimes I actually acted like one,' I explained to her.

'That's really cute,' she sympathised. 'But, hey, why don't you come to my house today? I mean, that's if you want really. I got free house and Amar's coming too. Should be a lot of fun, and we can get to know each other a little more,' she added.

'Yeah, it will be great! Thanks,' I added and headed towards my lesson.

The clock struck 1.20 p.m. and the hungry animals came rushing in; the queue for food was so long that it even reached the end of the small hall. I mean, yeah, the food served at school was nice, but on Mondays it was the best. They cooked the chicken tikka wraps—my favourite. To be honest, I wasn't really up for any food during lunch time; it was very bizarre, because I loved the wraps and had them every Monday. I had even changed a doctor's appointment to a later time so I could have the chicken wraps! Very abnormal, yeah, I know you think that. I searched around and tried to find an identifiable face beyond the crowd but couldn't see any of the usual faces until a hand grabbed my shoulder.

'Hey, bitch, no hello these days then, ey!'

Oh my god, even I couldn't believe who it was. It was Kiran—my best friend!

Kiran, aged sixteen, was a beautiful, gorgeous Sikh girl. I had met Kiran last summer at an Asian wedding—her family, her dad knew my dad through friends and, from that moment and time, she had become my other half. 'Hey, my special K!' That's what we call her—her nickname, you could say in one way. 'Hey, come to Amy's after school with me—everyone's hanging out in her house,' I added.

'Yeah, cool. Meet me on the runway,' Kiran shouted as she ran off with Rishi to the last period.

I was walking towards class, and I texted my mum asking her if I could come home late as I would be going to my 'new friend's' house.

Text: Mum

Hey, Mum, are you OK? Is everything OK? Ermmm . . . Mum is it OK if I go to Amy's house today for a couple of hours?

Kiran will also be there, and you know Mrs Green, right? Well, yeah, it's her daughter—Number 24 on our road. Text back soon.

From: Angel

Later, as the bell hit for home time, strong-blooded children hurriedly trampled out the school gates like a stampede of animals. About fifteen minutes later, George Hill School felt and looked like a ghost town. A cold shiver came down my spine.

'Hey.' A familiar voice came from behind. Of course, it had to be Amar.

'Oh, hey, you good?' I smiled.

'Yeah, yeah, standard and that. Let's roll off to my chick's yard.'

We both ran after each other. As we were walking towards the 71 bus stop, which took us to Amy's house, my mum's text came through:

To: Angel

No, get home now!

From: Mum

Following a good forty minutes' walk after I had said bye to Amar, because, of course, my mum didn't let me go, for reasons only God knows why! I reached my front doorstep and pressed the bell. I waited . . . Ten minutes later and still waited. No one could have been home as no one opened the door for me. I had no credit either, so I couldn't ring home or on my mum's number. I then figured to go next door to Mrs Sheila's house to see if I could use their house phone or something to get in contact with my mum. Mrs Sheila was a woman, who I have known my whole life, literally from the day I was born. My first sight was of her. What a wonderful, kind, sensitive woman she was! Honestly, she was like a second mother to me; actually, when times got tough on me, I considered her more of a Mum than I did for my real Mum. Like even right now as I'm telling you this, I'm considering Mrs Sheila as more as a mother. I knocked on her door and waited a good five minutes till she could get herself downstairs and open the door for me. She was getting quite old now and was finding it difficult to even hear me sometimes. Although she did look younger than her age, I mean for an eighty-four-year-old woman, she wasn't too bad.

'Hey, Auntie Sheila, have you seen my mum around? Did she give you any message to pass on to me?'

'Who's this at the door?' she screeched.

'It's me, Angel,' I said.

'Oh, *Beta*! (daughter) Come in, come in,' she said.

I stepped towards her lovely house and went straight over to the phone. I have always loved her house. I remember as a child, I always used to come over there to play with Mrs Sheila's daughters and family, but now they had all moved out and were getting on with their own lives. She had done a good job of raising nine kids! Pretty impressive! Don't you think?

'Mum, where are you? I have been waiting for you for the last fifteen minutes.' I tried to sound calm.

'Just stay at Sheila's house, and I will be home soon. Now don't ring and disturb me. I'm really busy here.' The phone hung; there was silence for a split second, and then it cut off.

I got so angry at her, I mean, why did she have to be like that? Why is she with her friends, and I'm with an old lady? Why? Why? Finally, I just got so frustrated that I just sat in the toilet and cried. For a good hour and a half, I just sat and cried. Why is my life so messed up? My tutor was also meant to be coming in like one hour, and I was in the toilet crying! You really have to be on my side on this one. I mean my mum was being unfair, right? Why couldn't she let me go? This is one thing I hate about my Asian family. They either over-exaggerate things or just take it wrong. They simply don't know when to stop!

# Chapter 3

## My House, My Home, My Habitat

I wouldn't really call my home a 'home sweet home'. It's more like 'home bitter home'. When I set foot in this household, my whole world changes; my emotions and feelings completely differ from how I feel when I'm out of my home. My mom is aged thirty-nine and is a businesswoman, Dad is aged forty-two and has an international business; Sonya, my younger sister, is aged fourteen and goes to school; Sameer, my younger brother, is aged four and loves football; Nikkie, my other sister, aged thirteen who I call the devil; and finally me, aged fifteen, a moody but sweet teenager. Now I know what you're probably thinking—a great family full of love and maybe very loyal and rich. Right? Actually, to be truthful, we are rich (I don't mean millionaires but close to it). I wear all designer clothes from head to toe. Clothing for me was never a big issue. Dad always wanted us to look good, so we always had the clothing we wanted.

We have six bedrooms in our house; the largest room is, of course, our parents' room, and I was given the second largest room. In my room I have everything a teenage girl would want. You name it, I got it. Yeah, again, you must be thinking, 'What a spoiled little bitch!' I might have it all—money, clothes, jewellery—everything. But one thing I don't have that many of you might do. I don't have a family; in person, they are with me, but in hearts they are somewhere else. It's actually quite heartbreaking. I mean, what's the point of having all this and not a family to share it with? I guess this is where I probably went wrong. This is why I gave my heart to a stranger's love, because I didn't get any from my own family.

'Food's in the kitchen. Warm it up and eat it, Angel, if you're hungry,' my mum, Mrs Khan, shouted from the living room as she was watching her favourite soap.

'Yeah, OK, Mum, thanks,' I shouted back to her, trying to get my voice heard over the TV.

I walked inside my room and just threw myself on my king-sized bed. All my teddies jumped, including the one he gave me. You're probably thinking who he is, yeah, I know, but I will explain it later on. For a good five to ten minutes, I stared at the ceiling above. The stars were hanging down as I tangled around with them. From the corner of my eye, green with a spark of hazel, I saw the heart drawn at the top corner of my ceiling. It was coloured red and white with the black ink on it. I can't remember the exact thing that was written on it, but I'm sure it had some kind of a name. Moreover, I didn't feel in such a good mood today; to be honest, I never have a good feeling when I enter this household. The atmosphere is always cold. Well, it's the way I feel; the surroundings and the atmosphere are almost like a graveyard.

I think it was about 7.00 p.m., when my dad stormed into the kitchen like a hungry lion. He demanded for food—my mom's rice, which is a kind of yellowish orange curry. It's delicious. I asked my mum to teach me how to cook, but I remember her saying no, because she thought I was useless at cooking. Like always, for my mum I was just a useless person—a useless daughter. How I wish now I had learnt to cook! I wish my mum had taught me how to cook! Had I known how to cook, I wouldn't be now living on takeaways and tinned food. Dad had his lunch and now was in a better mood. I heard our twenty years old staircase creek and knew straightaway it was him. I mean, no one else really talked to me in my household. Therefore, it had to be him.

A quick, sudden knock hit my door. Then his real deep voice came out gently, 'Can I come in, Angel?'

'Err, sure, Daddy,' I replied back innocently.

The next thing I knew, he was already beside my bed.

'Hey, Angel, don't ask to go to your friend's house again. You know you won't be allowed,' he told me frustratingly.

'Can I just ask why I'm not allowed as I don't know the reason to it, Dad?' I looked him in the eye.

'Because, we don't know what you do there.' He vanished into the long corridor.

You see how they over-exaggerate over these little things!

For ten minutes, I sat on my bed thinking why he had given me such a stupid answer or why was he so nice and calm. Did he have a plan? What was he up to? I got really curious that night.

Then suddenly, morning rose up and the beauty of the sun hit the rays of my window. A reflection of my gigantic mirror hit the wall. It was Saturday morning, finally weekend. I loved the weekends—hanging out with family and friends.

Meanwhile, my mum was telling our butler to clean around our house as she was having her friends coming over for 'tea'. She always referred to it as just tea, but they totally ended up doing more things than just drinking tea. Usually, they would just go out to a restaurant or stay home and watch a movie in the cinema room. It always ended up being the usual, same, boring thing. The most unfair thing was the obvious, of course, 'Why is she having so much fun and not letting me have a weekend too?' But there was no point in me asking her this question. I ended up with the same answer all the time. 'Because you're not married, and anything could happen to you.' That was the usual response I would hear from my mother. What is it with Asian parents and sex? Why is it that every time you ask them, 'Can we go out with so and so,' the reply you get 90 per cent of the time is, 'No, we'll go together and buy it.'?

I guess this all comes from the lack of understanding they have of us. You see, my mum never really fell in love with my dad but got married. My dad had, however, fallen in love with my mum and the marriage was arranged (the typical arranged marriage situation). My mum always thought negative of men, and she would say to me, 'Don't fall in love. Don't get yourself involved with boys. Wait till you are at least twenty-six to get married.' I'm assuming, she tells me all this because of her pessimistic past. The truth is that my dad cheated on my mum a couple of times, and until today she hasn't forgiven him. Isn't it funny how someone can hurt us over someone else, and we end up taking it out on others? I guess that's part of the human nature. We make our world revolve around one heart and yet we don't even taste the love from it. But surely not all men are the same? Are they?

Hmmm . . . love! What is love? I never really wondered about this whole expression of love. I mean, people say love will happen to you when the time comes, but I think people have to make the time come to them, you could say this is another aspect that people would say is destiny. Have you ever fallen in love?

*'I hope love never leaves you empty-handed,'* my auntie once blessed me with. I love my auntie Shanazia. She's more like an elder sister than anything; I mean, long straightened hair and glossy lips—that's more like sister material type.

Later that day, a letter came through from my school about my graduation day. I was terrified, scared, and mostly nervous. I mean, I loved school always and everything else about my school life was good, but I was never the good science geek or the great poet. I was just the average schoolgirl—my grades were OK and were good enough for my college. However, my grades were never good enough for my parents. Well, I'm guessing, you know what I'm talking about; well, at least, if you're an Asian, you know what I'm talking about. This whole 'you have to be a doctor or the must be a good lawyer.' The down fall of the Asian society is that they have to be the best; they have to put the family name up, and this is one thing that all the families compete with.

# Chapter 4

## No Trust

The ray of sunlight bursting through the exam room hit my light brown wavy hair. I remembered not having straightened it that day; I mean, there was too much pressure of the exams on my mind, and the last thing I would be worrying about would be my hair. My left hand was tensed already, and I could feel the warm friction pulse through my hand. Everywhere my eyes turned, all you could see was heads looking down. There were tensed faces everywhere, and it was so silent. The heartbeats of some students could just about be heard. I looked up and the clock just ticked 10.15 a.m. Then suddenly, 'Stop!' a teacher shouted. I knew that that was it, my last exam ever at George Hill School. All of my five years of hard work was put to the test. The screeching of the test papers still echoed in my ear as we left the exam hall. This could make me or break me.

'How do you think you did?' Kiran grabbed my wrist.

'Yeah, OK, actually. What about you?'

'Actually, I thought it was really easy.'

'Well, you would think that, wouldn't you? And besides, you always say that,' I told her as we were walking to our third lesson.

'Shut up!' her voice echoed down the hall.

As I was walking out the school gates and heading home, I remembered it was my birthday in exactly less than twenty days and the good thing was that, summer 2006 was on its way too. I hope we get some kind of sunny weather this year. We all know British weather! One thing, we just can't get enough of is rain!

'What are you daydreaming about?' Ayesha crept from behind.

By the way, Ayesha is one of my close friends. Speaking of rain, I remember when we were in year three, and it was pouring down with heavy rain and hail, and Ayesha and I had started to cry, 'funny times!'

Anyhow, I replied back to Ayesha, 'Oh, nothing, darling. It's just that I don't know what to do on my birthday, to be honest. I only got twenty days left.'

'Oh my god . . . only twenty days, and girl, you need to think fast, it's sweet sixteen.'

'Yeah, don't remind me, but I need to speak to my parents first and see what they say.'

I have always wanted a super sweet sixteen—it's every little girl's dream. I never really got any kind of special birthday. I just got the family gathering type. As a young girl, you would enjoy it, but every girl grows out of her little world. For Asians, it's the age of sixteen, that's what I thought, anyway. I walked into the kitchen, and our butler, Mr Hoover, was standing, and it actually looked like he was daydreaming. I think he snapped out of it when he saw me walking through the back door.

'Ms Angel, there's food on the table waiting to be served for you.' Mr Hoover pointed towards the dining room.

'I'm not hungry. Is Mum home?' I fidgeted with the blue tack in my hand.

'Mrs Khan is downstairs in the cinema room. Do you want me to call her up for you?'

'Ermmm . . . no, thank you,' I replied politely.

I quickly threw my school bag on the floor and ran to the basement, which my dad had rebuilt into a cinema room a couple of years back. I think it was for

Mum on her thirty-seventh birthday. I'm not sure, though. Mum was searching for Indian movies, by the looks of it, as I entered the room.

'*Salam* (hello).' I went towards her.

'Oh, you're back home, Angel. Have you seen Kajol's new movie?'

'Nope, Mum, but I think you had lent it to Afshan's mum on Tuesday.'

'Oh god, yeah, I did. I completely forgot about it! Never mind,' Mum added.

As she walked up the stairs out the cinema room, I followed her and tried to think of how to start my birthday conversation with her. But my mum, she had to be the wisest woman ever I had known, and like my dad always boasted about his cleverness to us, 'If a bird heads up and flies away, I know if it's a male or a female.' My mum, likewise, was one of those wise women. I think this could be partially coming from her scorpion blood. You know what they say, 'The blood of a Scorpion has a strong bond.' I guess that to me could be true from seeing my mother's strong bonds.

'Is there something you want to talk about, Angel?' she asked as we sat on the dining room table.

'No, Mum,' I lied . . .

'Actually, I'm lying,' I added, 'There is something I want to talk to you about . . . Mum, it's my sixteenth birthday in twenty days, can I have . . .' Before I could even finish off my sentence, my mum interrupted me.

'Angel, you know the answer and, besides, your father and I have something planned for you.'

Well, and there you had it. I had to kiss goodbye to my sweet sixteen. I was turning sixteen only once in my whole life and, even though, we are flooded with money, my mum still refused. This could be the trouble with my parents; they make their world too small . . . and my world too! And you know what the worse thing is? Changing my mum's mind was simply impossible—once you got your answer, don't bother to ask the same question again.

Never mind, I had my answer, and I just had to accept it. There was no changing it or fixing it; I just had to accept it. Whenever something like this happened to me, I just read the 'Serenity Prayer' my counsellor, Carol Lambert, gave me when I was in school.

'God, grant me the serenity to accept the things I cannot change, courage to change the things I can, and wisdom to know the difference.' And this, of course, was to accept the things I cannot change. As I walked in towards my room, I felt like someone had drained the blood out of me! I felt very gutted—real gutted. I mean, my mum didn't even give me a chance to speak; she didn't even hear me out, and the worst is, I had done nothing wrong to have been punished like this. This is one of those things that I might remember for the rest of my life!

For the rest of the day, I just stayed in my room and didn't even go down for dinner. All night in my bed I was thinking, over and over again about the plans I had of my party in my head. But slowly my eyes shut down, and I entered the dream world. I loved my dreams; they were always good, and they brought out the best of me. In my dreams, I always felt free, so free and wild, and as if I had the life of a real angel, and I really felt like an angel sometimes. Ever heard the expression, 'Dreams come true'? Well, I'll tell you something, they do. Dreams really do come true, especially mine. Every dream I have ever had in my life since I can remember has came true, if not the whole thing, parts of it have. This night was a very unusual night; my dream was very realistic, almost too real. In the morning when I woke up, I remembered the dream so clearly, as if it had actually happened last night. I remember, I was crying as I sat by a bench, and someone, cannot remember if it was a girl or a boy or whoever for that matter, came up to me and started to make friends with me and wipe my tears away. It was very unreal.

Early that morning I had felt so much better than the previous night; I mean, with that dream I had, I wanted to find out what it meant, what it was trying to tell me, or who was that person? I really wanted to know. I decided to phone Kiran and then connect Amar as well in the conversation like we always did. I told them about my dream and asked them what they thought of it. Surely they could at least give me some idea. They both just told me that the dream didn't mean anything and that it was because of the state of my mind which I had slept in. Yet I had a different feeling about this, and I asked, 'What about that person in my dream?'

Amar replied, 'Well, that is just someone who at that time and moment seemed like an angel who could make all things all right. But, Angel, you're an angel yourself, so stop bothering yourself with these things.'

I told them that it felt too real, I actually felt like I was there. Kiran then interrupted me . . . 'Don't worry about it, Angel. Some dreams do feel like that, but this doesn't mean anything.'

In the end, I agreed with them and tried to just ignore it.

'Thanks, guys, love you.' We all hung up.

That evening was so hot that I was in our swimming pool for like four hours. After I came out, dinner was ready. When I came in the dining room, everyone was already there. I just went in and sat down quietly without saying anything. Then worse came to worse. During dinner, my dad started a conversation about my birthday.

'You can invite two or three of your friends to come for your birthday. I will buy you a nice birthday cake, and you can have a fantastic birthday with your family.' My dad looked at me. I thought to myself, 'I have this fantastic birthday with my family every year. That doesn't change except the one difference this year was that I could ask my friends to come, and that's all.' I just looked down at my plate of Chinese food, which was my dad's favourite food, and I hate Chinese food. However, we all had to eat it as my dad had ordered it. Then I looked up at my parents, and I quietly replied, 'OK, I'll phone Kiran and Amar and ask them to come.'

When I replied, my dad suddenly dropped his fork and just looked at me puzzled.

Calmly he said, 'I thought you said Amar, which is a boy's name.'

I just stared at my dad confusedly; his reaction was very weird to Amar's name. I thought they knew about him and how great a friend he was to me. Then I finally replied after the long paused silent moment, 'Yes, he is a boy, Dad.' I realised then that I had made the biggest mistake ever by telling them about Amar. The dinner was completely ruined; my dad was going crazy, and I was trying to explain to my mum that there was nothing to it, but she wouldn't listen to me. She just looked at me and said, 'Move away from me, you bring shame to our family and to our name.'

Then she stopped and looked back at my dad. 'She has a boyfriend!'

When I heard the word *boyfriend,* I felt like someone has shot me right through my heart. At that moment, only I could understand the pain I was going through, for something like that could never be true in a million years. How could my parents think of me like that? I never had boys in my mind, not even for a second. I was turning sixteen, but I was not like other teenage girls. I just thought about girly things and babyish stuff. I mean, how could they think that about me and Amar? He was like a brother who had always been there for me. I finally looked up, wiped away my tears, and said softly, 'I will prove to you that you're wrong,' and just walked out of the dining room.

I went straightaway to my room and phoned Amar, connected Kiran, and told them everything that had happened. They both were as shocked as I was, then Amar started first, 'Don't worry, Angel. We will definitely come up with a good plan and prove them wrong. I promise you that.' Kiran also said determinedly, 'Yes, we will.'

That night, we decided the plan was going to be on. They both would come on my birthday without my parents knowing it, obviously, and then Amar would swear under holy Qur'an (the holy book for Muslims) that all I was to him was just a friend and a sister.

As my birthday was just seven days away, which meant that for those seven days, I was treated like crap. Meaning no one would talk to me, even when I tried talking to my little sister and brother, my parents told them not to talk to me as I would turn them bad like myself. That was the worst thing they did as they didn't know anything, but they wouldn't listen to me either. I just tried to keep myself away from all my family as much as I could.

Finally, the day came. It was my birthday (1 July) and I was sixteen finally, but it was the worst day of my life. I went downstairs to eat breakfast and expected to hear something like 'Happy Birthday, Angel' or something like that, but I got completely the opposite response—no one talked to me, and the worst thing was my little sister said, 'Oh, Mum, there's the girl who gave us the bad name.'

I just wanted someone to kill me at that moment; it felt horrible to hear it from my little sister, and my parents not saying anything at all. I just smiled at her, didn't say anything, and went back to my room.

Finally, the tick-tock of the clock struck 2.00 p.m. I looked up with a sad smile; it was time for my parents to be proven wrong. I was finally going to prove myself innocent, but at the same time, I felt horrible that I had to go through all that for something I hadn't done. Suddenly, I heard the doorbell ring. I was so terrified and happy at the same time. I heard my dad opening the door, and I felt a bit relieved as my dad had never seen Kiran or Amar, so he didn't recognise them. Then my dad's deep voice echoed, 'Can I help you?'

Amar began, 'Hello, sir, my name is Amar, and this is Kiran.'

My dad just took a deep breath and shouted my name, and before I knew it, I was in front of Amar, Kiran, and my dad. Then I replied politely, 'Yes, Dad.' He looked at me angrily and said, 'I told you there was not going to be a birthday party. What is the meaning of this?'

Before I could say anything back, Amar replied to my dad's question, 'We are not here for a birthday party, sir. We are here to prove to you that my sister Angel is innocent.'

I was in complete shock at Amar's braveness, I mean, no one talked to my dad in that brave voice, not even my mum. So my dad decided to let them in and listen to what they had to say.

Amar continued, 'Sir, we are both Muslims, and the most important thing in our religion is the holy Qur'an.' Amar looked around our living room for a few seconds like he was scanning for something, then he finally found it. He walked towards the table in the corner of our living room, picked up the holy Qur'an, and walked back towards my dad. Then he put his hand on the Qur'an. 'Sir, I swear on the holy Qur'an that I am holding right now, I have no kind of relationship with your daughter, except that of a brother and sister and that's all it is.'

In our religion, the only time you swear on the holy Qur'an is when you know for 100 per cent that you are innocent. My dad looked at Amar, and then at me in a much traumatised way as all the drama that had happened the previous night was over nothing. And the last few days were completely his fault, and his thoughts were wrong as well. He looked back at Amar and said, 'Thank you, son, thank you for this whole truth,' then he looked back at me 'Now what about that cake of yours? Should we cut it?' he said smiling at me.

I felt so amazed and happy that my dad finally believed me and knew that I was innocent. I stared at Kiran, then at Amar, and finally at my dad and answered very happily, 'Sure, Dad. Why not?'

I looked at my cake, then at my family, and then at Amar and Kiran too, and I thought to myself, 'What a crazy sixteenth birthday!' I prayed to God for those few days to never come back in my life as those were the worst days of my life.

'C'mon, Angel, make a wish and blow the candles,' yelled Amar and Kiran.

'Yes, Angel, blow your candles,' said my dad smiling at me. I looked at the numbers one and six glowing. I closed my eyes and wished, 'I wish I meet someone in my life who cares about me, loves me for who I am, tells me things that will make my days and nights, for me to come first in that person's life.' That was my wish . . .

There was a sudden knock at the door and, suddenly, I realised I was back in my university accommodation. I was back in my present. Kiran, Amar, and Sam opened my door and came into the room. Sam, Amar's girlfriend, and Amar, by the way, have been going out ever since college (two years). All three of them came in shouting, 'Come on, Angel, let's go out.' I looked at them and said, 'No, thanks, guys, I got a lot of work to do for tomorrow.'

Kiran came over, hugged me, and said gently, 'Don't be like that. You never go out. Listen, Angel, just forget the past and move on with your life. It's not your fault, so stop blaming yourself.'

I looked at her and laughed. 'It's not that. I really do have work to do. I have an assignment to finish for tomorrow, and I need to do my prayers (*namaz*) in a few hours.' All three of them looked at me in a very disappointed way and left my room. I did feel bad for not going out with them, but I knew I was not going to enjoy myself as I had too much on my mind, and how could I forget my past? It was all my fault. I looked at the time; it was about 6.30 p.m., so I had plenty of time to finish my assignment, and then do my prayers. I started writing my assignment and, not realising the time, I suddenly looked up and saw that the hand struck 8.30 p.m. I quickly did my Wudu (you do Wudu before you pray, so you are clean). I read the Qur'an for half an hour, and then did my prayers. After I finished my prayers and my assignment, I just looked around my room, and my favourite locket hit my eyes. I just stared at it and, suddenly, my past started to tumble in again.

Kiran and Amar left at about 8.30 p.m. I went upstairs to my room, because I was still shocked at what Amar and Kiran had done for me—they were amazing friends. Then I realised my dad was in my room, standing by my door. I looked at him and smiled. He came in and sat next to me on my bed.

'I got something for you, Angel.' He opened a very old box, and inside was a gold locket with diamonds on it. It was the most beautiful locket I had seen. Just on top of the locket was an old piece of paper, and then my dad gave it me.

'This locket belonged to my grandmother, who passed it on to my dad when he got married to give it to my mother. So when I got married, my mother gave it to me to give it to your mother, who is supposed to pass it to your brother's wife. But I want to change that tradition, and I want to give it to you. Do you know what this old paper is, Angel?'

I looked at my dad in fascination, thinking as to how I hadn't known about the locket before? I shook my head. My dad closed the locket, gave it in my hand, and said, 'It's a *taweez*, Angel. It has words from the holy Qur'an. You should wear it around your neck all the time so that it protects you from harm, evil spirits, and bad people.'

I was so thankful and amazed with my dad's present that I didn't know what to say. I just started crying with happiness. My dad hugged me and said sadly, 'What's wrong, Angel? Why are you crying?'

'Because I'm so happy and grateful with your gift, Dad. You broke the tradition just for me, but what about Mum? Is she OK with this?' I sobbed.

He wiped off my tears. 'Well, your mum is still mad at you as she still thinks there was something going on between you and Amar.' I couldn't believe what I was hearing. Why was my mum still thinking that?

'But, Dad, Amar swore . . .,' but before I could finish my sentence, I got interrupted.

'I know, Angel, but you know how hard it is to convince your mother.' I looked at him with sadness and resigned, 'I understand.'

# Chapter 5

## The Wedding/The Life Change

Wow! Finally my uncle was getting married. I was so happy. This was just something that gets everyone excited, especially Asian weddings. I'm not saying this because this is my culture or anything like that, but because an Asian wedding hits the roof and the tradition in itself is amazing. I remember when I was about five years old and my auntie was getting married. I was a young bridesmaid who held the Qur'an and my cousin Akki was the ring boy. It was amazing, and to this day, I remember it. However, when you're getting older, weddings start to mean more to you than when you were a kid; I mean, the whole wedding atmosphere starts giving you a sense of the whole idea of you getting older and the time for you to be the bride someday coming closer. Actually, it's a scary thought. Nope, not scary, it's terrifying! I mean, can you believe it that in about four to five years' time, I'm going to be a bride myself? '*Inshallah*!' as Muslims would say.

My uncle's wedding was less than two weeks away, and everyone was so excited and in their own world about how to look; it's kind of like, 'survival of the fittest' where everyone is in a competition to look good in their own unique style—a style that no one else should have. It was a very mad two weeks. The wedding hall had cancelled on us and our uncle nearly sued the company—that was a very big disaster. The wedding cake went wrong at the last minute, and the singer that my dad had called all the way from India, his flight had just got cancelled. Just so we are all on the same page, this was all happening three days before the wedding! My whole family was panicking! But me? It's funny because I was extremely happy as my dresses were all fixed. I had made sure that no one else had the same outfit as me, and I knew exactly how to have my hair done! It was great for me. Although I should have felt sad because of my uncle, but in one way, this was the first wedding I was going to and things were actually going well for me. Now all was left to happen was for the wedding to actually take place! Of course!

Just the night before the wedding, my uncle came to our house. I think it was about 3.30 p.m., and all my family were gathered in the living room. My uncle looked so sad that my heartbeat got quicker and quicker. Silence fell across the whole of our house. Tears nearly strolled down my uncle Assad's eyes; it was heartbreaking.

'I'm really sorry, guys,' he said with a hint of sadness in his voice. 'I'm so sorry, but . . .,' a long pause fell. Then he continued, 'I'm so sorry, but you will all be partying all night tomorrow!'

A sudden cheer came from everyone.

'Oh, that's fantastic, Assad!' my mum exclaimed.

'Yeah Sis'. I sorted everything out. From tomorrow, I will be spending the rest of my life with the woman I love.' He pointed at his future wife, Zainab, Auntie Zainab from tomorrow.

'Let's celebrate.' My dad came in with a bottle of champagne from the kitchen.

The whole night was full of joy and celebration. It was an amazing night.

Finally, it was the big day! The day we had all been waiting for! All the excitement we held in for was for this one day! Only this day! The excitement started to take over the whole of our house—especially mine. The wedding was going to start at five in the evening. I, on the other hand, had an appointment at 3.00 p.m., to be ready by 5.00 p.m. Our driver, Husain, took me to the best hairstylist and make-up artist in the whole of London. She was a six-foot-tall brunette with long straight silky hair. I had to say, she was just perfection from body to figure and figure to facial. She was the whole package.

'Hello, beautiful! I'm Victoria,' she introduced herself.

'I'm Angel,' I introduced back.

'Wow, I can see why your parents named you that!' She gave me a warm smile.

'Thanks.' I smiled back.

For the rest of the time I spent with her, she was telling me about her fantastic career and how she went to Hollywood. We chatted about nearly everything, and I told her a bit about my life. We both forgot about my hair, but the finishing product was out of this world! Before I could see myself in the mirror, Victoria told me to go and wear my dress first. I had to say, this was the most beautiful dress I had ever seen in my life. It was rose red with two patterns of silver crystal sequinned down the side of the dress.

'Wow! Tonight, you truly do look like an angel from heaven. You look so beautiful, so gorgeous,' Victoria said as she took out her camera.

'Please, someone give me a mirror.' I was so eager to see myself.

As soon as the reflection of the mirror hit me, my mouth dropped open. Ten minutes later, I still couldn't believe it was me. I just stared speechlessly.

'That's not me, Victoria,' I hesitated.

'Angel, you are *beautiful*!' she told me.

'I look so different . . . so . . . '

'Beautiful!' Victoria added.

'Thank you so much, Victoria. I wouldn't have looked so nice without your help, without your magic, and without you! Thanks a million,' I added.

'Don't thank me. This is what I'm here for. Now go and show your beauty off!' She pushed me towards the door.

When I stepped outside, Husain, our driver, didn't even recognise who I was at first sight.

'She is too hot.' A voice came from behind.

'Simply sexy.com.' Another added.

I quickly walked towards the car, and Husain opened the door for me. 'Beautiful!' he added.

'Thanks.' I shut the door.

It was quarter to five and the wedding hall was quite far from where we were at that time and moment.

'In twenty-five minutes,' Husain told me.

I managed to breathe after Husain told me that, because the traffic outside was crazy. Ten minutes later, I got a phone call from my dad. 'Angel, where are you, darling?'

'Ermmm . . . Dad, I'm just on my way. There is traffic, but we will get there in fifteen minutes. Don't worry about me.'

'OK, then, that's great.'

'Fifteen minutes?' I asked just to reassure myself.

'Yes, Angel,' he replied back.

For those good fifteen minutes, I was going through the song I would be dancing to as my uncle Assad was finally getting married! He was more like an elder brother than anything and, besides, he wasn't that old. Twenty-six isn't old. Is it?

Am so glad and happy that everything at the end went well and right for my uncle Assad. It felt like a real Indian movie, one like, when everything goes wrong, but at the end it is perfect. I loved it.

Dancing and music hit into the hall, and we were all having a great time. At about 7.30 p.m., the bride and the groom entered the hall. Everyone was gobsmacked! The couple was just *perfect*: right in every way and beautiful in every feature. The ceremony (*nikaah*) took place and now they were officially a married couple. The whole night was a success to all the Khan family. There was a smile on everyone's face. After food, my dad gave a quick speech, thanking everyone for coming, and wishing the couple a long happy life. The wedding was a blast of a night, and everything went just perfect! Well, that's what I thought, anyway. There I was by the double, cream, wooden doors waiting for all the guests to go and to say my goodbyes and thank them for coming, but it was my worst mistake, the biggest mistake of my life. What I was thinking, I don't even know, but my life changed at that very moment. I was minding my own business; actually, thinking about how great the night went—the laughter, the dance, and the happiness. But I didn't know that happiness wasn't written in my destiny (*qismat*). I never knew that from that night my life would be so bitter-sweet; if only I knew, if only.

'Thank you for coming, hope you enjoyed yourself,' I said to a woman in a very posh green-and-black silk dress; the woman looked to be in her mid-thirties.

'Thank you for your beautiful dances.' She smiled back.

There was his face, the face that ruined my life, the face that changed my life. He just stared at me at first, looked deeply into my eyes, and my heart felt like it was going to jump out my chest. The room seemed darker than it was. What was happening? I didn't quite understand.

'Thank you.' He pulled his hand out to say bye.

I thought, 'What do I do? Should I shake hands? Should I act like I didn't see him?' I was so confused. 'What would people think if they see me shaking a young boy's hand, especially Asian families?' I did something I shouldn't have. I put my hand out to him.

'Thank you for coming.' I looked down.

My hands were sweating, but it wasn't because I was hot; it was fear. In the palm of my hand, I felt a sharp pain; it felt like a cut. Paper! It was paper. Why was this boy holding paper in his hand and shaking my hand with it? I looked up, and he smiled at me. Knots began to knot in my stomach. I felt pain or was it fear again? I pulled my hand out quickly—something I shouldn't have done!

Suddenly the paper fell; the float of the paper felt like a bomb on the ground. My mum looked at me! She saw the paper, she saw the boy smiling at me, and she saw me shaking his hand! But was it my fault? I didn't know he was going to do that. I started to panic; my face was beginning to heat up, and I knew I was red. I felt sick! I acted like I hadn't seen my mum. I looked down; the boy pulled the piece of paper to himself with his left foot and walked off.

'What a fantastic night!' my dad shouted in happiness as we walked inside the house.

'Was it really?' My mum forced a look at me.

I looked down just staring at my feet. There was so much fear in me that I felt like I was going to throw up.

'Why don't you ask your "Angel" how she found the night?' My mum threw another look at me.

'Angel, how did you find the night, sweetheart?'

'Ermmm . . . yeah, actually, it was quite a night. I liked it very much,' I said quietly.

'You don't sound so convinced, Angel.' My dad pulled me in his arms.

'No, Da . . .,' but before I could finish off my sentence, my mum interrupted me,

'That's because your daughter is a cancer to this family, dirt, a disease!' she exclaimed.

My dad's arms dropped. Thunder hit my home.

'What?' my dad said confused.

'Dad, listen, please, it isn't like, Mu . . .,' I hurried the words out my mouth.

'Angel, *shut up*!' my mum shouted at the top of her voice.

I froze. I thought my heart stopped too. Actually, I felt as though my heart had stopped. All the blood in my body just froze.

'I saw her, Khan. I saw it with my own eyes, with the eyes Allah gave me. I saw this filth put shame in our family,' she continued to shout.

'What happened?' my dad asked.

My mum continued and, yet, I couldn't even defend myself as I was so shocked at what I was hearing.

'She gave her number to some boy there. She put her hand out and gave it to him, the paper dropped, and the boy took it away dragging his foot on top of it.'

Warms tears rolled down my cheeks and my heart broke. I felt it break into a million pieces. I fell to the ground. My mind blanked out.

'Mum . . . Dad . . . do . . . do . . . do you really thi . . . n . . . k that about me? y . . . o . . . u really think I would do that? You really think I would do that to this family? to this name? Dad if anyone, but I know you don't believe this, am your baby girl, Dad. Dad?'

Like a river flooding its way, my tears flooded too. I couldn't believe it. I couldn't believe they could even think of me like that, let alone blame me.

'Get out my sight, Angel.' A tear dropped from my dad's eyes. 'Get out.'

'Dad, please, D . . . a . . . d . . . '. I pushed out those last words.

My whole life changed from that night, my whole life. The room just blackened out. How could my God have brought this day on me? What had I done wrong? I was left in the dark corridor on my two knees asking God why? Why? Why?

# Chapter 6

## Ares

As the days, weeks, months went past, it felt like I was living in hell as no one spoke to me, looked at me, or even cared to what I was doing. The summer started in hell and ended in hell, but, at least, I was looking forward to one good thing—my results. I knew I had done well as I had revised really, really hard for them. '*Inshallah*!' as we Muslims say. Hopefully, I had done well—well, as in, good for my parents. Waiting all summer just for that one day which would determine the rest of my life and would finally win back my parents' trust.

Finally, the day came, 28 August, the 'result day.' I woke up at around 9.00 a.m., phoned Kiran and Amar, and told them to meet me outside our school at 1.50 p.m. as the results' collection started at 2.00 p.m. We planned to collect our results as early as possible, and then go and celebrate. I got ready and hurried downstairs and told my mum that I was going to collect my results. She looked at me as if I was lying and was going somewhere else. She didn't say anything, so I just left without even getting a 'good luck' from her. I arrived outside my school and saw Kiran and Amar; they were both waiting for me. I was so happy to see them as I hadn't seen them for over a month; the last time we had actually got together was in my uncle Assad's wedding. I ran and hugged both of them, and they hugged me so tightly, that for a split second, a feel of sympathy hit me. I was so excited to see them.

'We missed you so much, girl,' Kiran said smiling at me. I looked at both of them, thinking I was so lucky to have friends like them.

'You don't understand how much I have missed you both,' I said hugging both of them again.

'Come on then, let's go and get our fantastic results!' Amar exclaimed nervously.

Both Kiran and I laughed at Amar's nervous face as we were walking along the cold, moist corridor. As soon as we entered the school hall, we found it so noisy as if it was a stampede of animals—hungry animals craving for food; in our case, the food was our results. All the teachers were there. I was so excited to see everyone again, and then unexpectedly a horrible voice came from behind us. We turned around and saw Mr Harrison, the teacher we all hated. He looked at us with his violent smile.

'I wasn't expecting you all to come,' but before he could finish off his sentence, Amar interrupted him, 'Why, sir? Why would you think that?'

'Well, when you get your results, you will know,' he mumbled under his breath as he walked away and all three of us stared and watched him walk away. The knots in my stomach tightened hard. I felt as though a ton of stones were in my stomach.

'He's an idiotic teacher. Don't take any notice of him. I know we have done well,' Amar assured us.

Mr Harrison was always on our case as he absolutely hated us, but even till that moment then, we couldn't figure out why? It was very strange. We knew we hadn't done anything to him; we had always been pleasant towards him, yet he hated us. He even predicted us a grade 'E' in history, even though I had got an award for the history contest I entered last year. As we walked towards the vast queue where everyone was waiting anxiously to collect their results, we all knew one thing for sure. This was it! Our future was on those pieces of paper—it could either make us or break us. I was completely petrified, not for myself, but for my parents. They would kill me if I had done poorly. The thing is with Asian families—well, my family . . . bad for them is like if I get all Bs and one or two As, so this meant, I had to do exceptionally excellent. As our turn was getting closer and closer, my heartbeat started increasing rapidly. Then it was it.

Finally, our turn came. Amar went first to take his result, then Kiran, and last but not least, me. I was so frightened that I was shaking. I took the brown envelope, and the feel of the brown paper scratched into my palm. Even the teacher was looking at me weirdly. Amar and Kiran had opened their envelope straightaway; and they were both very happy about their results. I mean, I would be as well. Amar had got one A*, two As, and nine Bs. Kiran got two A*, two As, and eight Bs. I had bad thoughts in my head like always as I never thought positive about myself. I always thought negative about myself, and that's why I was too scared to take risks.

'C'mon, Angel, open it. I know you've done better than us,' Kiran said really excitedly. Obviously, who wouldn't be happy? Her results were great. I smiled at her nervously and said, 'No, I can't open it, you do it,' I gave the envelope to Kiran. She took it off me and gave it to Amar. 'Open it,' she told him.

As Amar was opening my results, I just closed my eyes and turned my back towards them. I was so scared . . . if the results were bad, my parents were going to think that I was messing around and having boyfriends.

'Wow, Angel, these results are excellent!' yelled Kiran. I stopped thinking and turned around with a confused face thinking they were joking.

'What?' I said oddly.

'Seriously, these are amazing results! Your parents will be thrilled,' Amar said smiling at me.

I took my results from his hands and looked at the paper myself. They weren't lying to me. When I looked, I couldn't believe my eyes. They were actually good: I had four A* three As, and five Bs. I was so happy that my eyes filled with tears.

'Hey, why you crying?' Kiran said as she hugged me.

'These are tears of happiness, not sadness,' I said to her as I wiped my tears away.

'You know, for the first time in my life, my parents will be proud of me,' I said smiling at both of them.

So we decided to go home first to tell our parents about the great results, then we were going to meet up by the cinema at around 5.00 p.m. I got home at 4.00 p.m. and ran straight to the living room where my mum was, and I shouted, 'Mum, my results are amazing. You are going to love me.' She looked at me furiously and yelled, 'Stop shouting!' I just froze in my place, and then she said in a raised voice, 'Give it to me. Let me see what you got.' I gave her my result thinking she would be very pleased when she saw it. She opened the envelope and observed vigorously for a few minutes.

'You think this is good? Which part? If you weren't too busy bringing shame to our family, then you would have done better,' she said as she threw the results in my face.

I was just so shocked thinking that it all was a dream and that it couldn't be real as I had done so well, but my mom was still not satisfied!

'But, Mu . . .,' before I could finish . . .

'Get out of this room. I don't want to see your face!' yelled Mum. 'First, you give our family a bad name, and then you come with these terrible results.'

I felt like every cell in my brain had exploded as I could not believe what I was hearing; I just fell on the living room floor crying.

'I said, get out of my face. You really think your fake crying is going to work on me?' she yelled.

I started breathing faster and faster and then suddenly I just looked up and reasoned with Mum, 'Why would you think I would cry fake? I never had any boyfriend, so why do you keep saying I gave the family a bad name?'

Mum just looked at me and said, 'Get out!'

'OK, fine. I'll go,' I said.

Calmly, I left the living room and went to open the front door to go and meet Amar and Kiran. My mum suddenly grabbed me by my arm and frightened the living hell out of me.

'I didn't say you could go out. I said go to your room.'

I just stared at her thinking why was my real mother doing this to me? I just couldn't figure it out and finally, 'fine' is all I could reply as I left the room and headed to my room. I threw myself on my bed and just started crying all over again. I was getting sick of this life where I got blamed for things I didn't even know about. Why Allah? Suddenly, I felt something moving in my pocket and then I realised it was my phone vibrating. I took it out of my pocket and realised it was Amar's call.

'Hello, Angel, where are you, man? We have been waiting for you for the last twenty minutes.' He was yelling from the other side of the phone.

After a few seconds, I burst out crying.

'I'm not coming, Amar,' I said crying as tears rolled down my cheeks.

'Angel, what's wrong?' His voice came through innocently, and I couldn't help but tell him everything. Amar said angrily, 'We are coming right now!'

'Please don't.' I just hung up and threw myself in my bed crying, and then suddenly I heard the front door open. I knew right then that my dad had come home. I was happy and scared at the same time. I was happy because I was hoping my dad would be pleased about my results, but scared as he might listen to whatever my mother said and make my day even worse than it is. So I decided to creep slowly out of my room to the top of the stairs and try to listen to what my mum would be telling my dad. I tried to listen what they were talking about, but I couldn't understand what they were saying; however, I knew my mother wasn't saying good things about me. Therefore, I decided to come back to my room as it was pointless for me to listen to what they were saying. I just sat on my bed praying to God that my dad would be pleased with me, and he would say something nice to me.

The bright afternoon sunshine hit my face as I wiped my tears away and listened to his footsteps coming up the stairs. I was just praying to God that my dad would understand me, and then suddenly, I saw the door opening and my dad entering my room. He came in with a very serious face, looked at me, and sat next to me. 'Your mum told me everything that happened, and I also saw your results,' my dad said calmly.

'But, Dad, you don't understand,' before I could finish off, he interrupted me and said, 'Don't try to explain anything to me, Angel. I do understand everything and the only reason your mum is upset with you is because she wants you to do well,' he explained to me.

I looked at him wishing he could understand what I was trying to tell him, but it was no point as he didn't. I stared at the brown envelope of my results that my dad gave me with my eyes full of tears, and I said, 'Can I go for a walk, Dad, please?'

'Yes, you can as it's early, but come back soon because it's getting dark,' he said as he walked out of my room. I wiped away my tears, grabbed my results, and walked out the house. As I left the house, my mum was asking my dad questions about why he had let me go out instead of punishing me. I just ignored everything I was hearing in the background and went straight to the high street. I was not even sure why I was even going there, but I knew that I had to get out that house. I couldn't take it any more.

As I entered the high street centre, I felt like everyone was staring at me saying things about me; I ignored everything around me and walked really fast towards the escalator. I was hoping Kiran and Amar would be there, but when I looked around, I couldn't see them anywhere. I thought, 'How come they hadn't come? Was it because of me?' As I was playing around with my weird thoughts, I didn't realise someone was behind me.

'C'mon, your results can't be that bad,' I heard an unfamiliar voice say to me. I turned around and saw this boy staring at me that I had never seen before.

I smiled at him and said, 'Trust me, they are bad . . . well, for my parents.'

'Hey, those beautiful tears are not worth some A, B, Cs, so don't waste them,' he said smiling at me.

I just stared at him thinking as to why that stranger was being nice to me. He had never seen me before and didn't even know me, but he was the first person in my life that actually understood me. It was very weird and strange, and it didn't make any sense to me.

'By the way, I'm Ares, and you are?' he said with a smile on his face.

'I'm Angel, but my family thinks the opposite,' I said smiling at him and thinking if my parents found out that I was talking to a stranger (a boy) they would kill me.

'Are you OK?' The only reason he asked that was because I think my face had become sad again as Amar calls it the 'sad face.'

'Yeah, I'm OK,' I alleged unhappily, but he could tell I wasn't. Suddenly, his friends who were waiting for him, I didn't even realise as I was so wrapped around my own sad world, they called out his name 'Ares, are you coming, man, or are you staying with your girl?'

I just looked at them thinking what a bunch of idiots they were to think that as soon as they see a girl and a guy talking, they assume that the two are in love! So stupid! Guys never change!

'Hey, don't worry about what they say. They're just being stupid like always,' he reassured after noticing the hurt expression on my face. I didn't say anything to him; I just smiled. Then he turned around to them and told them to go and said that he would meet them some other time. I just stared at him in confusion thinking why he was leaving his friends for someone he didn't even know; I mean, I had never seen a guy to be so nice and caring.

'Listen, Ares, you don't have to stay with me, they are your friends, I think you should go,' I said.

'No, no it's OK, you're more important,' he said as he was saying bye to them. This time he scared me as I wondered why was I more important to him than his friends. I mean, he knew them better than me, but the worst was that he had just met me. Then he looked at me and said, 'Come on, let's go and eat.'

'I'm sorry?' I said, confused as to what was wrong with the guy! He had just met me and was now offering me to go to a restaurant with him!

'Hey, listen, don't get scared. I know your results are good, so I think you deserve this and I'm not letting you go home all hurt and upset, so come,' he urged and winked at me with a smile on his face and walked towards the restaurant. I couldn't believe it! A stranger was nicer and more caring than my own family, and it was very hard to believe. He looked back towards me and saw I was still standing in the same place.

'Come on,' he yelled, so I decided to go with him.

We went inside the restaurant; however, I couldn't believe he was such a gentleman, you see—a guy pulling a chair out for a girl in a movie might seem like it's for real, and every guy doesn't do it, but, today, in real life, Ares was one of those guys who did. If you ask me if he was the perfect guy for any girl, then I would say that whoever ends up with him would be the luckiest girl in the world! I mean, there was nothing wrong with him; he was very good-looking, a gentleman and very caring. But this scared me a lot. He couldn't have been this perfect, thus there had to be something doggy about him. But what? Then, the negative side of my brain started to think; he could be a murderer or even worse a rapist. I started to panic then, but I think whatever I was thinking had started to show on my face.

'Hey, Angel, stop being so scared, OK, I'm not what you think. I'm, I'm just a normal guy who goes to the university and sometimes goes out with his friends.' I felt stupid and scared that he could be a mind reader and that he knew all the bad things I was thinking about him.

'I'm not any psychiatrist, but I can tell from your face expression that you are scared and that you thinking why a stranger is being so nice to you. Let me tell you something about myself. I'm not like the other Asian guys that as soon as they see a very good-looking girl start saying stupid things. To be honest with you, I don't waste my time running after girls or going clubbing. You're the first girl that I have started a conversation with.' He smiled at me as he continued,

'That's why my friends were being stupid as they couldn't believe it either, and the only reason I spoke to you was because when I saw you, you looked hurt, upset, and you didn't look like those kind of girls that run after guys. You were just standing there by yourself and straightaway I knew. Then I figured out that if a girl like you is alone at such a time, then there is a problem either with her family or with her very close friends. So that gave away that you were hurt, but the biggest clue was your brown envelope.' He smiled at me as he looked at the results on the table.

'So now that you got your explanation, can you eat your food before it gets cold and then I can drop you home as it's getting late? Your parents will be worried about you,' he said as he drank his Pepsi. It was great to have someone to talk to—someone who understood how you felt, even though he was a stranger. There is a saying: 'At worst times only your family will be there for you,' but in my case, that was not true. I have always realised that at my worst times, my family has turned its back on me, and I've only had my friends for support. Only this time, it was different. I was hurt, upset, and had no one, but suddenly a stranger came and helped me through it. Then I looked at Ares and thanked him a lot for guiding someone like me and for helping me. Suddenly, I realised that he did not have an Indian name. I knew he was Asian, but I wasn't sure what he was, was he Indian?

'Ares, I hope I'm not being rude, but can I ask you a question?'

'Yeah, of course, you can, but let me guess, you're going to ask me where I'm from, right?' he said, smiling at me.

I smiled back. 'Yeah.'

'You're of mixed race, right?' he asked curiously.

'Yes, I am,' I replied.

'I thought so, OK now, the answer to your question, yes, I am Indian but only half, and I'm half Afghani. Do you know where Afghanistan is?' he asked me.

Of course, I knew from the stupid marriage list that Dad had prepared for me and of course because I'm half Afghan. He had made that list for me to let me know who I could and couldn't get married to, and the most important thing in the list was that the guy had to be Muslim and at par with our status. This was very difficult, because there was no guy with both of the qualities that were on my dad's list; they were either non-Muslims with our class standard or Muslims with a lower standard than ours. So I finally replied back.

'Yeah, I do know where it is.' I smiled.

'My mum is from India, and my dad is from Afghanistan, so that's where I get my name from. But the best thing about being of mixed race is that you get to learn more than one language, for example I can speak four languages: Farsi, English, Urdu, and Hindi,' he said smiling at me.

'Well, I speak three of those languages you named,' I said really proudly.

'Let me guess, Farsi, Hindi, and English?' he said.

'Yes,' I replied back smiling at him.

'How do you know where Afghanistan is?' he asked me.

'Oh, my dad is from there too.'

'Oh, that is very good then, just like me, hey!'

'Yeah.' I smiled.

'Come on, Angel, don't give me that face. Didn't I tell that you look really pretty when you smile?'

I thought to myself that the guy was so sweet as no one had ever given me such a compliment before, so I decided to smile back at him. Unexpectedly, he said something really strange relating to my embarrassing story, which really frightened me, and I really do mean it.

'Now that you're smiling, tell me do I match your dad's list or not?' I couldn't believe what he said; I mean, what did he expect me to reply. I only knew him for the past two hours!

'Well, I don't know you that well, so I can't really say anything.'

'Don't worry, you will get to know me soon,' he alleged to me. But this time I could feel he really frightened me. I really wanted to ask him what he meant by that, but I didn't, because I thought it was rude to make him feel uncomfortable. Suddenly, I felt something moving in my pocket, and then I realised it was my phone vibrating. I always have my phone in my pocket as it's on vibrate mode all the time. I took my phone out of my pocket to see who it was and saw it was my dad's number at which I quickly said bye to Ares and ran out of the restaurant.

'Hello, Dad. I'm on my way home, is everything OK?'

'Yes, everything is OK. I phoned to say it's getting late, so come home.' His serious voice took over, but now that I think about it, my dad's voice was always serious and that could be the reason why we were all so scared of him.

'OK, Dad, I'm on my way now.' I put the phone down, not realising that Ares was standing in front of me.

'Hey, is everything OK? You just ran off without saying anything,' he asked, and at that moment, I suddenly realised how I had run off and hadn't even thanked him for making me feel better.

'I'm sorry. I didn't mean to run off like that. My dad phoned and told me to come home. It's getting late, and I didn't want him to know I was with a boy,' I said, smiling at him.

'OK, that's fine, come on let's go,' he said as he started walking towards the escalator. I couldn't believe what he was saying, I mean, was he trying to get me killed? What was wrong with this guy and why was he coming home with me? I was so confused, and then I looked up and saw that he was standing in front of me again.

'Stop thinking so much. I'm not going home with you. I just want to give you a lift home, don't worry, I'm not going to get you killed by your parents,' he smiled at me as he walked towards the escalator again. I felt so stupid; I mean, why was I so weird? I always thought negative, never positive, and how did he know everything I thought? Then I just stopped and told myself to stop thinking so negatively. Ares was half way down the escalator; he looked back and saw me at the top, and he smiled at me and walked towards the car parking. I followed him, but still you should know me by now, I had negative thoughts in my head. I just couldn't stop thinking negatively. We got in the car park, and I just stopped.

'Ares, listen you don't need to give me lift home. I live very close by, and I really don't want anyone to see me in your car. You know why.'

He stared into my eyes. 'So you want me to let you go home alone? That's not going to happen, and trust me no one will see you in my car.'

That confused me, well, 90 per cent of times I get confused very quickly, anyway. But I didn't understand what he meant by 'no one will see me in his car'? When we arrived near his car, only then did I understand as to what he meant when he said that no one will see me. His car windows were tinted black. Subsequently, he was about to say something like 'you understand what I mean now,' but I stopped him and alleged, 'Yes, I understand what you mean. Please don't make me feel even more stupid by repeating it.'

He smiled at me. 'OK, come on, let's go.'

I got in his car; however, I was shocked by how clean his car was. I mean, I have never seen boys maintaining such a clean and organised car. Even his CDs were placed in alphabetical order, so I could only imagine how clean his house would be! This was really impressing. Boys who are single and especially under twenty-five are usually very filthy and have filthy cars; however, I didn't know if he was under twenty-five, but he looked young.

'Do you want me to drop you a few blocks away from your house?' he asked me as he drove out of the car park. I looked at him thinking what an idiot, obviously! If you don't want me getting caught, then obviously you would let me go a couple of blocks away. I didn't tell him that as he would think I was being rude.

'Yeah, that would be great, thanks.' I smiled once more.

When we reached my house, well not exactly my house, but few houses away, I looked at him thinking that that would be the last time I was going to see him; however, I was so grateful to Allah (God) that he had sent an amazing guardian like Ares to help me through that difficult time.

Suddenly, Ares broke the silence. 'Why are you looking at me like this is the last time you're going to see me?'

All of a sudden my smile faded away; I mean, what was he trying to say? Was he hinting that he was going to see me again and again until I became his girlfriend or something? I knew there was something behind his kindness. I was right; no boy would be so nice to a girl unless he is after something! Well, he could forget that, because that was never going to happen.

'Hey, step out of your daydream! I will never do that to you, OK,' he whispered to me at the same time waving his hand in front of my face, and I snapped out of my weird world.

'Sorry, I don't understand what you mean?' I said like I didn't, but, of course, I did understand what he meant. However, I didn't want him to know that I did.

'Angel, you look like a very smart girl, of course, you know what I mean,' he hinted to me. I didn't say anything to him but smiled back. Subsequently, something else came into my head that I really wanted to ask him ever since I had met him, which was 'how did he know what I was thinking? Was he really a psychic?'

'Ares, can I ask you a question?' I asked him quietly.

'Of course, you can, ask me anything,' he said staring at me.

'How do you always know what I'm thinking? I wanted to ask you this since I met you. Are you psychic or something?'

He just looked at me and started to laugh really loudly, but I just looked down feeling so stupid by having asked a question like that. But then I think Ares realised, so he stopped laughing.

'Hey, I didn't laugh at you, so please look at me, and I'll tell you why.' I looked up at him and he started to explain. 'I laughed because you called me psychic. You really think I'm that clever? I don't think so, and the only person that can be psychic and clever enough is the beautiful girl sitting next to me.'

This made me smile, and so he continued, 'It's easy how I know what you're thinking, and you will be surprised when I tell you. It's your facial expressions.'

This confused me. Was he trying to say that I had a weird face? That was it. I needed to stop judging him and let him finish what he meant. If he said something mean, then I would complain and start thinking negatively in my head.

'Let me give an example,' he continued, 'like now I said facial expressions and your expression changed from a smile to confused looking face, and, no, I don't think there is something wrong with your face.'

I smiled and understood what he meant; it did make sense then as I thought about it, and I had, indeed, changed my expressions very quickly.

'I understand what you mean,' I said smiling at him.

'I think I should go now before my dad phones me again; however, I just want to say thank you, Ares, for everything you done for me. At worst times, you expect your family to be there for you, but mine wasn't. Although, I'm hurt a lot, I feel so lucky that I met a stranger like you who helped me through it. Basically, what I'm trying to say is thank you,' I mentioned smiling at him.

'You don't need to thank me. I didn't help an ordinary person. I helped an angel, don't forget. I feel, after today, my life will change forever, and don't worry, I mean, change for good not bad.'

Before I was about to get out of his car, I looked at my phone to see if my dad had phoned again, however, there was no connection on my phone which meant my dad must have phoned a lot of time. I think my facial expression must've changed again, because he asked me, 'What's wrong?'

'Uh, nothing, it's just that there is no connection on my phone. I don't know why?' I said to him gazing at my phone.

'Listen, I think this will help, give me your number, I'll phone you and see if there is any connection,' he suggested, so I handed over my number and when he phoned, my phone started ringing. I was so thrilled, because that meant I hadn't missed any of my dad's phone calls. Therefore, I decided to say bye to him and go home. I started walking away from his car, and I taken only a few steps when I just stopped as I had this strange sensation inside me that I might meet Ares once again. I couldn't figure it out why I had such an emotion and, therefore, I turned around to say goodbye for the last time as I knew what I was feeling was immoral. Nevertheless, I waved goodbye, and he did the same, yet I couldn't understand one thing: Why was Ares not that bothered about not seeing me again? Well . . . at least, he helped me and that's all that mattered to me.

When I arrived home, I could hear my mum complaining to my dad about me; I mean, I had been gone for four hours. I hope she hadn't been complaining that long. Before I had met Ares, I probably wouldn't have got home till my mum had calmed down, because I knew how she would react when she saw me. Yet, this time, I had these strange feelings of happiness and no regrets within me, and I couldn't figure out why. Was it because of Ares? I decided to go inside, although, I had promised myself that I was not going to let anything devastate my strange yet astonishing day. I opened the front door and entered the house. The extraordinary thing was that everyone had unexpectedly become silent, which I couldn't understand why. I mean, I didn't say anything, nonetheless, I realised one thing which was the best thing for me and that was to go to my room. I didn't even glance towards the living room as I knew if I did, someone would say something, but I realised I was wrong, for as I turned to go upstairs, my mum yelled out to my dad, so I could hear her voice too.

'See now that you let her go and see her boyfriend, look how happy she is.'

I just couldn't understand why she always accused me of having a stupid boyfriend! Such stupid accusing was not new. I mean, it had been going on since I was fourteen years old. I knew that my mum knew in her heart that I didn't have any intention of having a boyfriend, yet she still accused me. If she had said such things to me before I had met Ares then I would have probably started to cry and weaken down, but now Ares had made me realise that I shouldn't hurt myself if I knew what they said about me was not true. He had also said that God watches over who is in the right or wrong. I guess he was trying to tell me just to be happy; my happiness was more important. Therefore, this time I didn't start crying. I just ignored her and started walking towards my room. But I think this made her really angry as she screamed loudly, 'Look, she doesn't even care if I'm hurt or not. God knows what she must have done with that boy.'

This made me explode as to what was she saying? Done what? With which boy? None of the stuff she was saying made any sense at all. I really didn't want to argue back with her as I knew everyone would be on her side even if she was wrong or right. Calmly, I asked, 'Why do you keep saying I have a boyfriend? What boyfriend, Ma? Because of this family's name, I don't even talk to my friends who are boys as I don't want to let you down, but you still keep accusing me all the time. This is not new. It has been going on ever since I turned fourteen. Please stop this accusation, Mum. I can't take it any more. I assure you I have never had a boyfriend, but all you keep doing is forcing me to have one!' Tears started to trickle from my eyes, and I started to walk to my room. I could tell those weren't just tears. It was the hurt, the pain, and the sorrow all flooding down from my eyes. I was trapped. All I wanted in my life was for someone to love me, make me feel special, and make me feel like that I was worth something and not a poison in the family. All of this stuff you expect from your family, but mine never gave that to me; they always made me feel like an outsider, and I also think that I didn't belong to my family. As I was about to walk up the stairs, my mum screamed, 'So you think by treating me in that way, you will have a boyfriend, and I would be scared of you? How dare you! Go and have millions of boyfriends, see if I care. But I'll tell you one thing, you're not my daughter any more.' She slammed the living room door.

I knew there was no point in me telling her anything; besides, that's not what I meant as she would prove me wrong like always. Then, finally, my dad decided to say something, 'Listen, I think we should listen to what she has got to say. I don't believe that my daughter would give our family such a shameful name.' I felt so relieved that my dad believed in me; at least, I had someone on my side, but, like always, my mother could never accept being wrong as she shouted out.

'You believe her? She's lying, and all of those tears are fake, and how dare she try to teach me how to be a good mother!' She walked towards me and started pointing to my face with her figures and yelled, 'Who do think you are? Come on, tell me, are you my mother to teach me how to be a good mother? Or how I should talk to my child?' I just looked down, agreed to everything she said, and went to my room. I opened my bedroom door and sat on the floor with tears flooding down my cheeks. It felt as though an open tap had caused flooding and more flooding. I started praying to Allah (God).

'Oh, Allah, please help me through these hard times, please give me the strength to make my mum understand that I'm not as bad as she thinks. I need your guidance, Allah. I need someone in my life to help me. I can't do anything by myself.' At that moment, suddenly, my window opened and the wind started to rush into my room. It didn't make sense as the window was locked. How then did it open? I stood up, closed the window, and went to sleep. I knew in my heart that my Allah would help me through it. I didn't know how, but I knew one thing that he would send a guardian to guide me through my worse days.

# Chapter 7

## Faith of a Stranger

I woke up in the morning feeling absolutely horrible as I had had a horrifying dream, but then I realised last night wasn't a dream. It was real, and I hoped my mum had forgotten everything. It was weird as there had been a terrible storm the previous night, but the morning was bright and sunny. But what can one expect in England? The weather here is always strange; one minute it's raining, and the next it's sunny; it never made sense. Anyway, I picked up my phone to see what time it was and there was a text on my phone. I smiled to myself thinking I had missed my two best friends so much; we hadn't spoken in weeks now. I unlocked my phone and realised that it wasn't Amar or Kiran. It was some number that my phone didn't recognise.

> Good morning, hope last night you slept well.
> Just wanted to say be happy, don't worry about anything.
> So tell me, Angel, do you still remember me?
> Take care ☺

I looked at the number a few times, but I still couldn't figure out who it was. Maybe, it was Amar or Kiran playing a joke on me, then I realised we never did that to each other after the disaster that had happened last time! But who was this person? If this text had gone to someone else's phone, they probably wouldn't care, but me, I was different. I had to find out who it was. I just sat on my bed thinking who knew what had happened yesterday besides my family, but it was obvious it was not my own family as I knew they couldn't care less about me. Then, suddenly, I realised who it was, and I was just about to shout out his name, but I knew if my parents heard it, I would be dead. They would have proved that I had been with a boy the previous night. I'm not saying that there was something going on between us, but as you probably know my parents by now, they would think that straightaway. I was so pleased to know it was him; however, I got confused thinking how did he get my number? Here it comes! My negative brain thinking as though he was a spy! At that moment, I just stopped myself from thinking negatively and decided to reply his text:

> Morning to you too ☺
> Well, I wasn't happy, but I got your text I'm.
> Of course, I remember you, how can I forget?
> But can I just ask, how did you get my number?
> Anyway, how are you?
> Take care

I sent the text and just sat on my bed waiting for him to reply. There was no point in me going downstairs then as I knew I wasn't wanted there and because everyone would then be having breakfast and by my going there would ruin it for them all. I figured to myself I would wait till everyone finished their breakfast, and then I would go and eat. At that moment, unexpectedly, my phone started to vibrate; I saw that it was his text and straightaway I read it.

> Why, weren't happy? What happened?
> Come on, tell me, it will make you feel better if you share your pain and I don't think you still know who I'm as you haven't mentioned my name
> Tell me, what's my name? I'll tell you how I got your number when I phone you, OK?
> Take care

I couldn't figure out why this guy was so nice to me? At that moment, I realised my wish had came true; perhaps, Ares was my guardian that I asked from Allah (God).

> Nothing really, just my mum got mad at me.
> It's complicated and I can't explain everything in text
> Why do want me to say your name? I know who you are
> But if it makes you happy, I'll say your name: Ares
> OK, if you want to phone me, phone at 2.00 p.m. OK
> Take care

When the text went, I checked the time, and it was 11.30 a.m., which I wasn't expecting as I always woke up so early and especially never this late. At that moment I realised that I had gone to sleep last night at maybe 2.00 or 3.00 a.m.; I remembered just crying so much. I got up and had my morning shower and figured that then was the best time for me to go downstairs as both of my parents would've gone to work, meaning no one would say anything horrible, and it meant I could eat my breakfast in peace. Hence I went downstairs, and as I entered the dining room, everyone just stopped eating and started to stare at me like I was some kind of a murderer who had just entered the courtroom. The thing was, if my parents were not home to make me feel down, there was always someone else; in my case, my sister Nikkie. I really hoped they would understand me and be on my side, but obviously, I was wrong. I should have known they would listen to my parents, especially my mum. On the other hand, I can't blame them as they were just children, and children tend to listen to their parents over their sister; I would have done the same too.

My sister Sonya who was fourteen years old, I loved her so much as she was my rock at my worst times. If it wasn't for her, I would have gone crazy. Whenever I was hurt, she would be there for me and would tell me that everything would be OK as we had got each other. I trusted her more than anyone in the world as we shared all our secrets, and the most amazing thing about Sonya was that even if you threatened to kill her, she would never tell anyone my secrets. However, that's what you would expect all sisters to be like, but, no, you're wrong, and I was wrong too as my other sister was pure evil and, trust me, I mean, evil. After Sonya was Nikkie who was thirteen years old but acted like a thirty-year-old evil woman. She's like a younger version of my mum; however, my mum had the right to tell me off as she was my mother, but what right did my youngest sister have in telling me off or making me feel down. I remember, when she had started being evil to me at the age of ten or eleven. I mean, at that age you would expect a little girl to play with dolls and bake brownies. However, not her; she used make plans how to make my life full of misery, although, now when I think about it, I don't blame her as kids that age only listen to one person and one person only . . . their mother! I knew Mum never meant whatever she said about me back then and even now in front of the kids, yet they were kids, and they didn't understand that she used to say things in anger, so they just copied her. So when Mum started saying awful things in front of the children, like how much she hated me and that how I had given our family a bad name and many other such things, Nikkie then began hating me and always tried to make my life a living hell.

But Sameer? He was my world. I loved him so much. I don't think any of us could image a second without him. Well, the first reason was obvious as Sameer was the cutest, and the second reason was that he was the youngest in our family, only four years old. Hence when my mum used to and still does say stuff in front of them about me, it was then that the seeds of hatred were sown in my sister Nikkie's heart. But as for Sonya, though, she knew all the stuff that Mum was saying wasn't true because she and I shared everything. Sameer was far too young and still was to understand anything Mum was saying, so this meant that the only person left was Nikkie who did understand things but chose to hate me, anyway. I'm three years older than her, but still she swears at me. When she's mad, she throws whatever's there in her hand towards me; however, the worse thing is that when I tell Mum, she doesn't forbid her from doing that, instead, she tells me that it was my own fault and that I deserved it. Nevertheless, sometimes my dad listened to me when I told him, so it was good to have him, even if it was sometimes.

Before I was about to join everyone on the table, Sameer pulled my hand and whispered to me 'Angel, I missed you. Where were you? You and I usually have breakfast together.'

I felt so blessed from Allah (God) that I had a brother like Sameer. Finally, I answered him back, 'I'm sorry, *Jaan* (I call him that because I love him so much; it means life). I had a really bad headache last night, so I couldn't go to sleep till late. I promise it's not going to happen again, OK?' He agreed with me and gave a hug.

When Nikkie saw my happy face it meant that my day was wonderful while Nikkie's was hell as she couldn't stand to see me happy. Seeing me happy absolutely killed her. She had to do something to make me feel down so that she could feel good. It has always been like that, and I still don't know why. It was better for her to give up as it didn't matter what she did or said as long as Sonya and Sameer never stopped loving me.

She had once told Sameer, with the intention of making him dislike me forever, that I had said about him, 'I hate him, and I'm not his real sister.' Nikkie thought that she had done a brilliant job and that Sameer would hate me from then on. However, the complete opposite happened as he ran to Dad crying and telling him to tell Nikkie to stop saying mean things about me. That was a great day as she got grounded for a week. But the worse thing is that she still hasn't given up. Having to see Sameer hug me and tell me he missed me, utterly killed her.

As I sat down, she muttered underneath her breath but loud enough for me to hear it, 'Well, if you hadn't messed about with lots of boys last night, then you wouldn't be tired, would you?' That was it! I had had enough of her. I stood up and yelled on the top of my voice, 'Listen, you piece of shit, Mummy is not here to stick up for you, so if I was you, I would shut my mouth or otherwise I'm going to beat the hell out of you, and I mean it. Do you understand me?' She just stared at me thinking 'wait till Mum gets home,' and, finally, she decided to leave the dining room, and I sat down. It felt extremely amazing to get all that out of my system as she had been annoying me since the previous night. However, then I couldn't say anything as Mum was already mad at me. When I looked at Sonya to see her reaction towards me, and I saw she was smiling to me, it made me feel even better.

First time in months, I actually enjoyed breakfast; therefore, I decided I was going to wake up late every morning as then my parents would not be home, meaning no one would tell me off. After finishing breakfast, Sameer suggested that Sonya and I should watch *Bob the Builder* with him. He utterly loved it, but the good thing was that he was not like the other kids who watch the DVD till the end; he would fall asleep ten minutes into the DVD. As a result, every time he asked us to watch a 'baby movie' with him, we both used to say yes straightaway, because we knew it never would get to the end. As we were going up the stairs to Sameer's room, I whispered to Sonya, 'I got something important to tell you.'

'OK, tell me after Sameer's "baby movie."' And we both started laughing as we always teased Sameer about his baby movies. At that moment, suddenly Sameer turned towards us and very suspiciously asked, 'Are the two of you making fun of my films again?'

We both answered at the same time, 'No . . . No . . . Of course, we are not.' Then we looked at each other and smiled. We couldn't watch it in living room as the devil (Nikkie) was there making plans how to make my life even worse than it was, and she was watching some top ten chart stuff at the same time which I never watched. Anyway, we put the DVD on and started watching it in Sameer's room. After a few minutes, we saw that Sameer was getting tired and one bit in the DVD would prove to us if he had fallen into deep sleep. It was when the Bob, the builder, said, 'Can we fix it?' and Sameer always answered back saying, 'Yes, we can!' So we waited for that bit to come; however, we realised that he had fallen asleep already. Sonya then switched the DVD off, and I put Sameer in his bed, and slowly we both crept out of his room. When we came out his room, we both felt so relieved that he didn't wake up as any slight movement usually woke Sameer up very quickly.

'Let's go to my room,' I whispered to Sonya, and we walked slowly towards my room so Sameer wouldn't wake up. As we entered my room, Sonya demanded me to tell her what was so important which I wanted to tell her. I looked at her confusedly and said, 'I didn't know you were that desperate to know. You acted like you didn't care.'

'Yeah, I know, that's one of my best qualities which annoys people a lot,' she said really proudly.

'Well, guess what! I don't get annoyed cos I'm used it,' I reminded her.

'OK, OK, you win, now come on tell me, please,' Sonya begged me. So we both sat on my bed, and I began telling her everything that had happened with me and Ares. Sonya and I usually shared everything from whatever that happened in school or anything else for that matter. I can go on forever with the list.

'Remember, when I went out yesterday, well . . .,' before I could finish off, she interrupted me.

'I knew there was more to that. I mean, how can you go out for like four hours by yourself? You met someone, didn't you?'

'Hello! It's my story. Can I finish it off or are you going to finish it for me?' I alleged, smiling at her.

'OK, sorry, please continue,' she said putting a cute face to impress me and, weirdly, it always did work. Anyhow, I told her everything from how he helped, made me understand that I shouldn't punish myself so much, and that I should always keep myself happy. I even showed the texts he sent me, and the first question she asked me was so predictable, 'Is he hot?' I looked at her thinking, 'Didn't you listen to any other things I was saying?'

'What about all the other stuff I said?' I asked her.

'Oh, sorry, Angel. I kind of stopped listening when you said he's a guy, and all I could think of was if he is hot or not,' she alleged jokingly.

'Are you serious? You actually stopped listening to me?' I asked.

'No, I'm just joking. Of course, I listened to everything, but come on, tell me please. Was he good-looking?' She begged me. On the other hand, to be honest, I didn't know about his looks as that day I was so hurt that all I cared about was someone who could make me feel better and that's what Ares did.

'I don't know, Sonya, I didn't really look at him the way you do when you see every other guy on the street,' I reminded her.

'Heyyy! What you trying to say?' she demanded me.

'I'm only joking with you. But seriously, I didn't really notice his looks as I was too upset that day as you know.' I jogged her memory.

'You know what, Angel, I think he was a Good Samaritan who walked past, saw you hurt, and offered to help you. You should be very grateful to Allah (God),' she said to me.

'Yeah, I'm and that's how I saw it as well,' I replied.

'Don't think too much about it, OK? Anyway, I'm going downstairs to get something to eat. Are you coming?' Sonya asked.

'No, you go, but whatever you're going to have, bring me some as well, please,' I said looking at my phone as it was almost 2.00 p.m.

As soon as Sonya left the room, my phone started to vibrate, and when I looked, it was Ares. I answered the phone expectantly knowing it was him who was on the phone. I didn't say anything till Sonya was downstairs. Finally, I said, 'Hello.'

'Hello, are you busy? Do you want me to phone you back later?' Ares asked me politely.

'No, no, it's OK. I am not busy, I just waited till my sister went downstairs and, by the way, thanks for being so patient,' I replied back.

'So tell me how you are. Are you happy?' Ares asked me, and I smiled to myself as no one till then had cared about how I was or if I was happy or not. It feels absolutely amazing to have someone like that in your life. I finally answered back.

'I'm OK, thanks for asking. Well, my day wasn't good, but after your texts it was quite good. You know, Ares, you're kind of my good luck charm, because since I met you, I have become happier, and I now understand that life is worth living and not crying and getting hurt 24/7,' I said.

'Don't say that, Angel, please. I haven't done anything, you were happy today as you believed in yourself for once, and all I did was remind you that,' he said.

I guess he was right as most of the time I used to think negatively; therefore, thinking positive for once in my life had paid off. Before he could ask me any more questions, I asked first, 'OK, tell me now. How did you get my number?'

He first laughed and then answered, 'Well, try to remember what happened that night. You said there was no connection in your phone, hence I asked you to give me your number . . .' Before he could finish off, I interrupted him.

'Ooooohh, yeah, I now know how you got it. I can't believe it you planned all this, didn't you?'

'Yeah, of course, I did. Did you really think I was going to let an Angel go?' he said proudly. I felt so special that he thought so well about me. I wish my parents thought the same, especially my mum. To be honest, I got kind of mad at him too as that night I was very upset with the intention of losing a very good friend, and he acted like he didn't care by not asking for my number. But, in fact, he cared more about losing me than I did as he took my number. So I started my complaining, 'I hate you. I'm never going to talk to you again as you really upset me that night.'

'Really? Why did you get upset? Wait a minute. Was it because you thought you will lose me forever?' Ares laughed.

'I'm not answering any questions, just remember you hurt me, OK,' I said moodily, but in actuality I wasn't; I just wanted to see his reaction.

'OK, if I upset you, then I apologise. However, remember one thing, Angel, you will never lose me. I will always be with you and that's a promise I'm making to you,' he spoke in a very calm voice. It didn't make any sense to me as to what he meant and what he was trying to tell me by saying 'always.'

'Let me tell you one thing about myself. I never tell anyone about anything I do, I just surprise them when they least expect it. OK, now let me give you an example, it will make more sense. Like I took your number and acted like I didn't care about not seeing you again. However, I knew I wouldn't have lost you as I had your number, but you didn't know that. So now do you understand what I mean?' he finished off with a question.

'Yeah, I do understand what you mean, but, Ares, sometimes you could really hurt people,' I said to him.

'Don't worry if it comes to that. I will tell them. OK?' He made me understand. 'Now come on, tell me what happened last night which you couldn't explain it on text.'

So I told Ares everything as he knew half of the stuff, anyway and, therefore, there was no point of me hiding it from him. Ares was a really good listener, and he just listened to everything I told him, and finally he said, 'Don't worry about it, Angel, everything will be OK. Trust me on this. I do understand it's not your fault, but you need to know the only reason your mum says that kind of stuff to you is because she loves you so much. She cares so much about you that she doesn't want you to have bad name. So don't take anything to heart. OK?'

I guess he was right; however, I wished Mum didn't say all those horrible things in front of everyone, because all she was doing was making herself look bad and making the kids lose respect for me. The negative thing about all this was when Nikkie repeated everything to my face, it hurt me the most.

'I guess you're right, Ares,' I said.

'Remember one thing, Angel, whenever you need someone to talk to about anything, I'm here for you. When you tell me things, think as if you're telling yourself. As I will never mention it to anyone, and I swear to you on Allah's (God) name,' he assured me.

I didn't know what to say to him, but I knew one thing, which was that I had found an amazing friend who would be there for me, no matter where life took me.

At last, I replied, 'Thank you, Ares, I'm a very lucky person to have a friend like you in my life. Anyway, I have to go now as my mum will be home soon.'

We both said goodbye to each other, and he promised me that he would phone me the next day.

As I put the phone down, Sonya came into my room with the food. I think it was tuna sandwiches.

'So, did he phone?' Sonya asked me as she put the tray down on the table.

'Yeah, he did,' I said to her.

'And what did he say?' she demanded me. I started telling her everything which Ares and I had talked about and after listening very quietly, Sonya looked at me and said, 'This guy really cares about you. However, one thing I can't figure out is why? I mean you said you only met him two days ago, so how can he like you in such a short time?'

'Exactly, that's what I don't understand either. However, Sonya, I really don't want to lose him as he is an amazing friend. Although, I will try to find out what is his plan,' I told her.

We both were talking about random stuff when, suddenly, Nikkie came into my room and just stared at us for a few seconds.

At last she said, 'Mum will be home soon.' Basically, she meant that when Mum came back, we were going to be dead as she then could do whatever she wanted when Mum was around.

'Well, then, that's good. You should be downstairs thinking of ways how to make my life miserable, don't you think?' I said to her sarcastically.

She just stared at me with an evil smile on her face and answered finally, 'Miserable is a good word which you used. I'm going to make your life worse.' And after having said so, she left my room. I looked at Sonya and said, 'There is seriously something wrong with that kid. I mean, she's only thirteen years old, but she acts like some evil soul of a thirty years old woman who has possessed her.'

Sonya started laughing, and I continued, 'Seriously, she's like one of those women whose husbands have left them, so they become all weird and start to make other people's lives hell, just like themselves.'

'Stop it, man,' Sonya said laughing at the same time.

'What? She is . . .' I said laughing at her, and we both started laughing really loudly. All of a sudden, we heard the front door open, and we both yelled to each other, 'Mum's home!'

I knew then that our fun for that day was over as Mum had been mad at me since last night, and I knew it was going to last for at least a week; her anger always lasted long. Also, on top of that, stupid Nikkie was behind my back, and I could feel that something horrible was going to happen that night. Anyway, Sonya went downstairs, because if Mum found out that she was with me then she would be in big trouble as Mum had told her to stay away from me or else I would turn her bad just like myself. I still didn't know how I would mess her up, but according to Mum, I would. I just stayed in my room as I knew my mum didn't want to see my face; it was better for me to go downstairs at tea time. At around 7.00 p.m., my dad came home, and Sonya came upstairs to tell me to come down for dinner. Before I entered the dining room, my mum had been talking and laughing really loudly; however, as soon as I entered the dining room, she just unexpectedly went quiet and looked at me. I felt like I was some kind of burden in her life who had just entered the dining room. I absolutely hated it when she did that, because she made me feel so guilty for something I hadn't done. Anyhow, I went towards my dad and quietly, I said, 'Hey, Dad.' Therefore, I repeated myself and said to Mum, 'Hello, Mum.' However, she completely ignored me and didn't say anything to me, so I just sat down.

When the food was served, it looked like Turkish food, I think, and it was obvious that Mum had ordered it as she was the only one who liked Turkish food. I waited for everyone to take their food first and thought I would take mine later as I didn't want any more arguments. When everyone took theirs and started eating, I saw there was a bit left for me and, therefore, I took all of it. After a few minutes, Nikkie started complaining to Mum that she hadn't got enough to eat and that she was still hungry.

'Take some from her plate, she's got enough,' Mum spoke like I was some kind of servant in that house. She didn't even say my name and referred to me as 'her.' I didn't say anything as I remembered what Ares had told me, and he was right. Mum had the right to say whatever she wanted to me.

Hence I replied, 'Yeah, sure,' however, out of nowhere, Nikkie yelled out, 'I don't want hers, it's disgusting.' This really made me mad as I was eating with a spoon and so what she was saying was beyond my comprehension.

'What do you mean, it's disgusting? I'm eating with a spoon, not like you with your hands, and if you don't want it, just say so. I don't think there is any point of being so rude,' I answered her politely.

'Well, you told me you would never eat my food. You would only eat Sameer's and Sonya's, so why should I eat yours?' she said stupidly. I looked at her with disbelief.

'What are you talking about?' I asked, but before Nikkie could answer, all of a sudden, Mum yelled out, 'Shut up, Angel! What the hell is wrong with you? Can't you stand seeing us happy for one day? You caused a drama last night and ruined everyone's night, and now you're doing it again. Just tell me one thing, what do you want from us?'

I just froze as I couldn't believe what Mum was saying. Why was she saying those things to me? I felt like every chamber in my brain was shutting down and any second I was going to die. I wish that was true; so I could have died right then, because I couldn't take any more lies. Then I realised that it had probably been Nikkie's plan and that she was right. 'Miserable' was a good word I used.

'Mum, please, why you are saying all these things?' I asked her almost in tears.

'Angel, it's enough. Don't you dare talk over your mother,' Dad said in a loud voice. I just shut up as I knew there was no point in me saying anything as everyone was against me, well, except Sonya and Sameer, of course.

Mum got out of the dining room at the same time and yelled out, 'I can't even have my dinner in peace because of this poison in our family. I wish from Allah (God) that you leave this family quickly so we can be in peace.' It didn't make any sense as she had already finished her food; I was the only one who hadn't. After she had left the dining room, Dad stood up and motioned to everyone to leave the room. Therefore, Nikkie was the first to get up with a smile on her face. From her smile I knew she was thinking that she had won once more. Before she was leaving the room, she told Sameer to come; however, Sameer refused to go with her. He yelled out, 'No, I don't want to go with you. I want to be here with Angel.'

'Sameer, go,' Dad said in a deep voice, and Sameer knew that if he didn't obey Dad's command then that would be the biggest mistake of his life. When

Dad said something, it always had to get done. No one dared refuse his order; it had always had been like that. Therefore, he left the room with Nikkie. I just sat there looking down on my plate, and then I felt a warm hand over mine; when I looked up it was Sonya.

'Don't worry. I'm there with you always,' Sonya whispered to me. I was so grateful to Allah (God) that I had Sameer and Sonya in my life as they were always there for me when my worst times hit me, especially Sonya; she made my world. I was in deep thoughts thanking God when, unexpectedly, a deep voice came into my ears, and then I realised it was Dad calling Sonya, 'Sonya.'

We both knew straightaway that it meant to get out of the dining room; therefore, she went with Dad leaving me by myself. As soon as I saw there was no one in the room, I just started crying and asked God, 'Why am I being punished like this? What did I do wrong in my life that I deserve this? I never asked for anything before, but one thing I'm asking now is I want my family back. I don't know where or when I lost them, but I want them back. Please, Allah (God) give me the strength to win my family back, please.'

I put my head on the table, carried on crying, and wished this was all a dream and that I was going to wake up any minute, but I knew it wasn't a dream. After a few minutes of crying, I decided to go and apologise to my mum. I knew it wasn't my fault, and I hadn't done anything. However, at the end of the day, she was my mother; if it wasn't for her, I wouldn't be in this world, and she had the right to be mad at me. I wiped my tears away, got out of the dining room, and started walking towards the living room. However, as soon as I got in the corridor, I started hearing loud noises and laughter. It didn't make any sense to me as how could they have been mad one minute and be laughing the next moment. As I got closer to the living room door, I saw this happy family who were having fun and enjoying themselves. I couldn't believe what I was seeing; I was crying in the other room and no one cared! It was like I didn't exist, that I was not a part of this family. I realised then that my family was really a happy family but without me. I had to face the truth one day; I was not wanted there, and I shouldn't be there. I always thought Mum said horrible things to me, because she was mad at me, but then I realised it was because she really did hate me, and she really wanted me gone. I was crying, but I couldn't figure it out why tears were coming from eyes; I just sat down in the corridor and started crying again. This time I wanted to know from Allah (God) why he had placed me in a family that didn't want or need me. They hated me so much that they couldn't even be in the same room as me? I do understand everything. Allah (God) did have a reason behind it, but it didn't make sense. What could've been the reason behind this? As I was continuing crying, I heard Mum telling Nikkie to do something; however, I couldn't hear what she was saying exactly. But one thing was clear. Nikkie was coming out of the living room; therefore, I quickly got up and ran up the stairs to my room. When I got inside my room, straightaway I got into my bed, but before I went to sleep, I prayed to God to please help me to get rid of that nightmare and bring back my old life.

The warm breeze of the moist air hit my dark green emerald-coloured curtains lifting them up high; the twitting of the birds hit my ears gently. As I opened my eyes, I felt like there was a huge stone on top of my head; of course, that was not possible unless Nikkie had done it, but then I would be dead. Therefore, I realised it was just a really bad headache, so I just ignored it and started searching my bedside table for my phone. When I looked at my phone, I saw there was a text and, straightaway, I knew it was Ares. This was because I was banned from talking to Amar and Kiran as Mum thought they were bad influences on me.

> Good morning, Jaan (life).
> Hope last night was better than the other night.
> If you want to talk to me, just give me a call or if you don't have any credit, give me a miss call and I'll phone you back
> Take care ☺

When I finished reading it, I knew straightaway that he had made my day by sending such a nice and caring text like that. However, one thing which confused me was, since when had I become his *jaan* (life)? As it was a romantic word and the only people you would call *jaan* (life) were the ones who meant the most to you. But, in a way, it was really sweet of him to think about me like that. As I sat up, I saw Sonya sitting at the bottom of my bed, and she was staring at me like she knew something about me.

'What?' I said to her with a smile on my face.

'You know it, that's why you're smiling. Was the text from your lover boy?' she yelled out.

'Shut up!' I whispered to her as I didn't want the devil (Nikkie) to hear it and cause another drama. I decided to show Sonya the text and see what she thought of it. She observed the text for a few minutes and finally answered, 'If you want me to be honest with you, Angel, I think this guy really likes you as he has only met you once, and he cares so much about you. I mean, it can't be friendship. There is something else behind it and that something else is "like" or perhaps even "love."' In a way, she was right; however, I refused to believe her as Ares didn't look or ever sound like that.

I only had seven more days to go, then college would start and everything would be OK. Well, that's what I was hoping for. I had decided from the previous night's experience not to have dinner with everyone till everything calmed down a bit and also try to stay away from Nikkie as I knew she would do anything to get me in trouble. I didn't want to tell Ares everything that had happened in our house, but somehow he just knew from hearing my voice that there was something wrong, and it was really weird. Also, when I told him everything, it made me feel a lot better, and he always tried to cheer me up and made me forget about everything that had happened. Well, just till Mum came home again. I tried most of the time not to go downstairs when Mum and Dad were home as I knew something would happen, but even when I didn't go near them I still got told off. Most of the time it didn't make any sense; however, I just ignored the whole thing and hoped one day Allah (God) would make everything better again. Unfortunately, as the days went by, things got worse and worse, but I was thankful for one thing and that was Ares. If I didn't have him, I would have gone crazy by then; he made me understand not to take everything to heart and that one day everything would be OK.

The day finally came; I was so excited that I was going to go to college the next day. Well, there are two reasons: first, because I was getting away from all those arguments and, secondly, as I hadn't seen Kiran and Amar for two weeks, I missed them so much. I fixed my bag and my clothes and decided to go to bed really early as I was going to wake up early the next day. Before I went to sleep, I wished from Allah (God) to make my first steps in college full of happiness and success.

# Chapter 8

## College/Meeting Ares

The first thing I did as soon as I got out of the car was to call Kiran, and I told her to meet me outside the college gate with Amar as I had missed them so much; I knew it had only been two weeks, but it felt like it had been two years. Oh yeah! I forget to say, Dad dropped me off to college every day as Mum said she couldn't stand to see my face for that long, which was only five minutes. However, obviously for her it must feel like five hours or something as she couldn't stand me. Although after college, I was allowed to walk home as we only lived twenty minutes away from my sixth form, and I was really glad as I wanted to spend as much time with Kiran and Amar. I walked towards the college gate, and I saw both of them waiting for me, and the next thing I knew I was hugging both of them and that was how much I had missed them.

'Oh my god! I missed you two so much. I can't describe it,' I yelled to them, still hugging both of them.

'Are you kidding? We missed you more,' Kiran yelled out.

'We really wanted to phone you, but then Kiran said we shouldn't as you might get into more trouble than you already are,' Amar said hugging me.

'I've got so much to tell you two. You probably wouldn't believe me,' I said to them.

'OK, it's almost 8.30 a.m. and the lessons will start in a minute, so we'll talk about it at break time, yeah?' Amar said to me smiling. I smiled back and hugged him. 'I missed your sweet words so much Amar.'

'Hey! What about mine? I always say more nice things than Amar,' Kiran demanded. We both laughed and, finally, I answered as we started walking inside the college, 'I know, babe, I don't need to tell you this as you know it.' As soon as I entered the college, I just stopped, closed my eyes, and re-wished my wish from Allah (God). We all went our separate ways as we all had picked different subjects except mathematics and so our tutors were different as well.

When I entered my tutorial, I realised I was a bit late as everyone was staring towards me. I just stood there and said quietly to my tutor, 'Sorry for being late.' She just looked at me and smiled. 'It's OK, go and sit down.'

I looked around for a good place to sit; I didn't want to sit at the back as a bunch of idiotic boys were there, and they were making signs towards me which I couldn't understand. All of a sudden, I heard a girl saying to me, 'Hey, come and sit next to me.' I was so relieved to hear her voice; otherwise, I would have ended up sitting with those idiots at the back. When I sat down next to her, she introduced herself to me.

'I'm Samantha, but please call me Sam as I hate the name Samantha, and I still can't figure out why my parents named me that.' I smiled to her and introduced myself to her as well.

'I'm Angel.'

'Wow, you got such a cool name! I would love to have your name,' Sam said to me excitedly. I think we were talking quite loudly as our tutor looked at us, gave that look meaning be quite, and she said, 'Girls!' at which we both went quite and finally started to whisper.

As our tutor was explaining how the college worked and was giving out our timetables, it was then I realised how cute Sam was. She was sweet, kind, and very pretty; I mean, there was nothing wrong with her, and I got a feeling she would be perfect for Amar, if he agreed. My meaning by 'if he agreed' was that he had really bad experiences from his previous relationship, and he had said to me and Kiran that he would never go out with any girl till he finished university.

Suddenly, I was woken up from my daydream by the bell; I realised, it was break time, and I was as glad as I wanted to introduce Sam to Amar and Kiran. When Sam and I entered the canteen, it was so packed that we could hardly walk. I started searching around the canteen to see where my two best friends were. However, I couldn't see them anywhere; maybe, they were still in their tutorial, so we decided to go right to the end of the canteen hoping they would be there. As we pushed and shoved through the crowd and finally when we got to the back where they weren't there, I was so disappointed as I couldn't see them anywhere. When I looked at Sam, I noticed she was smiling; I gave her a funny look and at last asked her, 'Why are you smiling?'

'Nothing,' she said continuing to smile. Suddenly, I felt something around my waist; it felt weird, and it was moving closer to me from both sides. When I looked down at my waist, I saw it was someone's hands, and I suddenly turned around to see who it was. As soon as I saw it was Kiran, I hugged her. 'You idiot, you scared the hell out of me.' She started laughing with Amar.

'That was the plan.'

'Shut up,' I said to both of them at the same time, and I hugged Amar. At that moment, I realised Sam had just been standing there quietly, and I had completely forgotten to introduce her.

'Ooooohh yeah, by the way, this is Sam, and we both are in the same tutorial,' I introduced her to them. Amar just said hi from where he was standing, but of course, Kiran, like always, said hello and started asking her random questions to see if she was good enough to be our friend. She always did that with every person we met and then she decided if he or she was good enough to be our mate; the scariest thing was that she always ended up being right and, therefore, we just agreed with her.

As Kiran continued with her weird questions, I looked towards Amar with a smile on my face; he gave me a funny look and finally spoke, 'What? Why are you looking at me like that? Come on, Angel, tell what you want, because I know what that look means.'

'Nothing, so now I'm not allowed to look at you?' I said putting a serious face so he would take me seriously.

'No, it's not that, but I know you always want something when you look at me like that,' he said staring suspiciously at me.

'Ohhh! OK fine, I'll tell you. What do you think of Sam? Don't you think she's cute?' I said with a cute innocent voice so he would fall for it.

'Ohhh no! No way are you two doing that to me again. I don't think anything of her. I still haven't forgotten that other girl you set me up with,' he sneered.

'OK, OK, calm down, but come on, babe, I didn't set you up that time. I didn't even like her when I first met her. It was Kiran, and we both know that,' I said calmly. 'So please, do this for me. I promise you will thank me in a few months' time,' and by then, I put on the 'sad face.'

With an annoyed expression on his face, Amar said, 'OK fine. What do you want me to do?' With the biggest grin on my face, I whispered, 'Go and talk to her. Get to know her, please, Amar.'

'Fine,' he said in aggravation as he walked towards Kiran and Sam. I was as pleased with myself as I knew this would work out perfectly; Sam and Amar was an ideal couple.

While I was standing there being pleased with myself, I felt something move in my pocket, and then I realised it was my phone vibrating. Anyway, when I looked at my phone, I saw it was Ares; I just started smiling to myself and finally answered the phone.

'Hey, are you busy?' the first question he asked me.

'No, no, no why?' I answered with confusion.

'It's just that you took a long time to answer your phone, so I thought you might be busy,' he told me.

This was so awkward. How was I supposed to tell him that I was so excited to see his phone call? I was just daydreaming about him! It was not that I liked him or anything, it was just that when I talked to Ares, everything became all right, even when it was not.

'I didn't feel my phone vibrate, I'm sorry,' I said, feeling embarrassed.

'So how's your first day in college?' he started the conversation.

'Well, I don't know yet, because it's only been couple of hours. However, I might start to enjoy it after a few weeks.' All of a sudden, I saw the time and it was time for my next lesson. Before I got a chance to tell him that I had to go, he knew straightaway.

'Angel, I think it's time for your lesson, we'll talk another time. Go to your lesson now and take care of yourself, bye.' I thought to myself how sweet he was because he cared so much about me, and he had only known me for like less than a month.

'Bye *Jaan*,' I said and quickly cut the phone off. I did that because I was expecting it to feel a bit odd and for Ares to say something weird, because I had called him *jaan* for the first time, but I had a feeling he liked it. When I turned around, I saw Kiran standing in front of me with a big smile on her face; I gave her a smile back. 'What?'

'Bye, *Jaan*? Did you just call someone *jaan*?' she said doing my expiration. 'Seriously, man, there is something going on between you two, because the way you talk to him it gives it away. Girl, I t-h-i-n-k someone is in l-o-v-e,' she said dragging the words out. But I was confused as I hadn't realised before. I mean, I had never realised it; I always considered Ares as a guardian who was in my life to help me through my bad times. That's all he was to me. Or was he?

'Come on, Kiran, it's nothing like that, I call you and Amar "*jaan*" as well, and he is the same as you two to me,' I said still thinking about what she had said.

'So you see Amar as a brother and me as a sister, hence you see him as a brother, right?' she said grinning. 'Besides,' she continued, 'you called me and Amar *jaan* after two years of knowing us, not like this prince of Persia whom you've only known for a month, and he has already become your life. I know I don't make sense to you now, Angel, but just think about it tonight and ask your prince, and then it will probably make more sense to you,' she said putting her arm around me.

As we started walking towards Amar and Sam, I just couldn't stop thinking about what Kiran had said to me. I mean, yes it was true that I had only known Ares for a month, but this was also true that I couldn't stop thinking about him; I mean, he was always on my mind, like 24/7. However, what did all this mean? It couldn't be love. Or could it? Suddenly, Amar woke me up from my daydream by shouldering me and whispered, 'She's pretty cool you know, Angel.'

'Who's cool?' I said all confused and still waking up from my daydream; Amar looked at me with a puzzled look on his face and whispered again, 'Angel, what world are you in? I was talking about your friend Sam, the one you introduced me to,' and then suddenly it hit; I was finally awake.

'Ooooohh sorry, babe. I'm just a bit tired,' I lied. 'Didn't I tell you that you would like her?'

Sam and I were in the same class for biology. However, Amar and Kiran were in different classes, but they both were mad at us with the purpose of why were we in the same class. I mean, it wasn't our fault. While we entered the biology lecture room, I was still thinking about what Kiran had told me and tried to figure out what had she exactly meant.

When the lecture started it was so boring; I mean, ten minutes passed and it felt like ten hours. Basically, it just dragged on. The lecturer was like a tape with the stop button broken. So I just started thinking about Ares again; all of a sudden, I heard my name, however, very vaguely. Then it got louder and louder at that moment, and I realised it was the lecturer calling me.

'Are you with us, Ms Khan?' he asked me in a deep voice.

'Yeah, I am,' I answered quietly.

'So what do think? Is it yes or no?' he asked me.

I was so confused as to what he was talking about; yes or no to what? If he was asking about my concentration, then, yes, I was daydreaming and, no, I wasn't listening to him. But, obviously, he wasn't asking about that. Suddenly, I felt something pinching my arm and a notepad being pushed towards me. I looked down and it said, 'Say yes.'

'Yes, the answer is yes,' I said proudly as I knew it was right.

'That's correct, Ms Khan, but next time, try to be a bit faster,' he said as he continued with the lecture.

Whispering to Sam, I said, 'Thank you.' I felt so relieved and thanked God. If Sam wasn't next to me, I would have been so humiliated.

After college, when we all met up, Sam told Amar and Kiran about my first and most embarrassing biology lecture. After she finished telling them, all three of them started laughing so loud that a bunch of guys were going past us, and they asked as to what was so funny. Except that the worse thing was that they were about to tell them; however, before they began, they looked at me first to see my reaction, and all three of them realised that if they did, I would have probably killed them. Therefore, they stopped themselves and Amar told them, 'It's nothing.' As we continued walking, I yelled out to them, 'Well, I'm at least brave enough to do that. I don't see you three to do this.'

When I got home, there was no one. Well, just the usual people like the staff, but that was it. It was only 3.00 p.m., so I ran straight to my room and phoned Ares. I didn't phone because I missed him or anything like that, I just rang with the intention of being kind. I just really wanted to know if he understood what Kiran had meant. When he picked up, he started off first even before I could say anything, and he said the strangest thing just like Kiran.

'Angel, I'm going to tell you something, but you tell me if you think it's true or not OK.' I got so scared as I didn't know what he meant; I mean, what was he trying to tell me which required my opinion? Therefore, I finally replied really quietly, 'OK, go on tell me.' He took a deep breath and started with a weird sentence.

'You know, Angel, you and me are not just friends any more. It just feels like we are more than that.' I didn't understand at all what he meant. Of course, we are more than friends, we are really good friends. I think that was what he meant. But still I asked him just to make sure if I was right.

'What do you mean?'

'I mean that normal friends are not like me and you. For example, I can't stop thinking about you, you're always on my mind, and if I don't talk to you for at least four or five times a day, it feels like I have lost something. Now you tell me, do you think normal friends are like this, and what about you? Are you the same as me?'

I didn't know what to say; he was right. I was exactly the same as him.

'Yeah, I'm the same. But what does this mean?'

'I don't know, Angel, but I never felt like this before for any one. I just can't imagine a second of my life without you. However, I don't know why I'm like this.'

The worst thing was that I felt exactly the same. So what was I supposed to say to him?

'Don't worry about it. I think if you see me then you will feel better and understand your feelings much better,' I said to him like I knew what I was saying, but I had no idea. After saying goodbye to him, I just lay down on my bed and started thinking if what we felt for each other was love. As people do say, love happens when you least expect it, and it happens with the person that you never expect to happen with. But was it love? Was I really in love? Is this how love feels like? Because if it was true, it was really hard as it hurt too much. I wanted to ask someone who had been in love before so that they could make me understand. But who? I couldn't ask Amar as he had never been in love; he just messed about with all the girls he had been with. As I was in my thoughts, I could hear Sonya's voice from downstairs, and for that reason, I decided to go downstairs instead of stressing myself here.

When I came back into my room at around 10.00 p.m. to sleep, I noticed there was a text on my phone. I knew straightaway that it would be a message from Kiran, Amar, or Sam as they would probably be feeling bad for having made fun of me the other day. Conversely, I was wrong as it was Ares, and he had texted the weirdest thing ever.

Text: Hey, Angel, hope you good.
Just wanted to know what time you going to meet me
Tomorrow? x

I didn't know what to think; what the hell was he talking about? I never said I wanted to meet him, but did I let him believe to think that I did want to see him? I thought about it for a few minutes, then suddenly I realised I had actually, when I had spoken to him earlier in the day.

'Ohhh god! What am I supposed to say to him now?' But then I thought I should go and see him because all the confusion would be sorted out like he said. I had a massive gap the next day, anyway, so I decided to see him and, therefore, I replied saying:

Text: Hey, I'm good, thanks.
OK, I'll meet you from 12.00 a.m. till 2.00 p.m.
Is that good for you? Let me know, x

The next thing I know, my alarm clock woke me up at 7.00 a.m.; still half sleep, I started searching for my phone on the table to switch the alarm off. I was about to switch off the alarm, when I realised I had got a text from Ares.

Text: Good morning! ☺ Yeah, that's fine.
I'll see you at twelve.
Take care. x

I was excited and terrified at the same time; I knew I had seen him before, but this time I was seeing him for a different purpose, and that was what that scared me the most. What if someone saw us together! Suddenly, I just stopped myself. What the hell was wrong with me? Why did I think so badly about myself? It was not like I was going to do something bad with this guy, no way, not in a million years. I was just going to sort the confusion out, that's all.

'What are you doing sitting there? Are you planning to go to college today or not?' Sonya shouted as she walked into my room. At that moment, I realised that she was right; I was sitting on my bed for the past god knows how long, thinking negative thoughts again. As a result, I quickly got up and started getting ready because I was getting late.

When I got by the gate of the college, like always, Kiran, Amar, and now Sam were waiting for me. The first thing I said before saying hello or giving them a hug was, 'I got something to tell you all.'

It was very funny as they all got really scared. I smiled and said, 'Don't worry, it's not a bad thing. Well, I don't think it's bad, anyway.'

I started explaining everything to them about me and Ares; after I finished, Kiran and Sam both agreed with me, but Amar didn't. He looked at me with a serious face.

'I don't want you to get hurt as you've got enough problems in your life already, and I don't want that to get worse. So if you ask me, I would say, don't go,' he said seriously.

'Yeah, but, Amar, that's why I'm going so there would be no problems in the future and to get rid of this confusion as I don't know what I feel for this guy. All I know is if I see him today, it will help me a lot to make my mind up,' I explained to him while looking at his new top. Finally, I made him understand. At first, he agreed, on a condition that one of them could go with me, but then I told him if any of them came, then Ares would never tell me what was there on his mind. It was hard at first, but we managed to convince Amar to agree with us.

All I was thinking in my head was how I was going to talk to him? It was obvious that it was going to be different from the first time I met him due to my feelings and his being different now. I hated it when I thought too much, because then I started to think strange and stupid things in my head which really scared me. That's it! I told myself. I was not going to think so negative any more. He was going to come for an hour, and we would talk nicely and everything would be fine. Ooooohh, then I wished it was twelve noon as I was thinking positive for once in my life, and if he came, everything would work out perfectly. At least, it was lesson time then, so I didn't have to think about Ares, and the best thing was that it was the chemistry practical and not the boring biology lecture in which I was embarrassed.

The only thing I hated about the practicals was the beginning as the teacher talked for so long that my thoughts usually went back to my Ares and to the perfect world which I had created in my mind. As she was talking, I didn't know about what, but I knew it was something to do with the practical, but I was in my own world. All of a sudden, I heard someone calling my name in the background; I quickly switched off my thoughts of Ares and turned back to the normal world to see who was calling me. But it was waste of time as it was the fat girl setting next to me. I know I'm being mean and I'm not usually like this, but trust me, if you were in my situation then you would have said the same thing.

'Yeah, what's wrong?'

'No, nothing is wrong, just wanted to ask if you are working with me,' the poor girl said nicely. I looked at her thinking, 'You brought me back from my daydream to ask me this!' Stupid girl! But obviously, I didn't say this as it wouldn't be nice; therefore, I answered her back, 'Yeah, sure.' But I couldn't understand why she got so happy about it; it's really scary as you get to meet very weird people in this world.

At last the practical finished, but the closer it was getting to meet Ares, the more scared I was getting. The clock struck 11.55 a.m.; this meant in five minutes' time, I would be face to face with Ares. God! I'm going crazy. I should stop thinking so much. 'I'm just going to concentrate on what the teacher is saying and not think about him.'

'OK, you all can go now, but don't forget your homework for next Monday,' the teacher yelled out as everyone had started leaving before she finished.

'Yes, Angel,' she said to me. I looked at her thinking, 'What do you mean 'yes, Angel?' At that moment I realised there was no one in class, and it made sense why she said that. I gave her a smile. 'I think I should go now.'

She nodded her head and followed me out of the classroom. I walked as quickly as I could into the toilet just to check how I looked in the mirror and ran back out to the college gate. When I got there, I couldn't see Ares anywhere; maybe, he hadn't arrived yet or he might have forgotten. However, I could see this really nice two-seater black car, Audi, coming from the distance. As the car was getting closer and closer, the guy who was driving it began to look very familiar. He looked like some actor! I stopped staring towards his direction as he was getting closer, and he probably thought I was some kind of weirdo; hence as he stopped in front of me, I looked away. I thought that was my lucky day as the guy I had found was so good-looking.

'Are you shy or you don't recognise me, Angel?' Of course, I did recognise him; it was just that I never knew how good-looking he was. All of a sudden, I realised all this I was saying in my head, like always not to him. At last I turned around towards him, and he gave me that cute smile again. I thought to myself, 'This guy's so *fit*!' Ooooohh my god! Trust me; he was very good-looking: styled black hair, brown eyes, and fair skin. He was wearing a yellow tee shirt with one ring on his right hand. A chain with his name on dangled down from his neck; the matching bracelet too was dangling from his wrist.

Suddenly, I heard someone whispering behind me. I turned around to see who it was, and it was the three people I should have expected to be. I couldn't believe it; they were spying on me, and the person who was whispering as usual was Kiran. I tried to listen to what she was saying and I heard, 'Is this Ares?

Cos if he is, he is too fit! No wonder, Angel wanted to meet him. If I was in her place, I would have done this a long time ago.' She smirked. They all then disappeared back inside the college.

'Ares? You're Ares, right?' I pointed at him, then realised that pointing was rude.

'Now you realised I'm Ares or did your friends over there tell you who I was? Cos if they hadn't told you, you would've embarrassed yourself by asking me who I was.' He laughed.

I was so embarrassed, I didn't know what to say; he was right, but still I was not going to make myself look stupid in front of him.

'No, no, it's not that.' I didn't make myself look only stupid, but I made myself look like an idiot. Why did I always do that to myself? I never learnt from my mistakes. What was wrong with me?

'Anyway, don't worry about it. Come on, let's go, we can't talk here,' Ares said. As he started driving, I didn't know how to ask him 'where are we going?' He just continued without saying anything, and I didn't bother asking either. I thought to myself, 'Let's just enjoy the drive.' I fully knew I was safe in his car.

I started staring at him and realised how different he looked from the first time we had met. No wonder, I didn't recognise him; everything was different about him, in a good way, of course. His dark black, with a hint of wave, hair was much longer than before. When I say long, I don't mean ugly long like all the way down to your shoulders. His hair was nice long and easy to comb through with your fingers. I didn't usually like yellow-coloured shirts, but the one he was wearing then, I thought I was in love with yellow all over again. The shirt looked amazing on him with the collars up, and his beard was neatly trimmed with the line—it was just wow! That's all I can say; I mean, before he didn't have it. I think all guys should have their beards shaped in pencil line. To be honest, I had always being a fond of guys having the pencil line on their beard, and it didn't matter how ugly the guy was as long as they had the line; to me then it was perfect. However, if the guy was as good-looking as Ares, then he would look extremely attractive with the line! He didn't even have the full line, it was a half way one, but still he looked really attractive. All of a sudden, I noticed he was staring at me from his rear-view mirror, and I quickly looked away so he wouldn't notice that I was staring at him.

Finally, he went into the usual shopping centre car park, the one where we had first met, and he parked the car and turned the engine off. I just didn't know what to say. I didn't know what was wrong with me. As strong as I thought I was in my head, it was much more difficult than being in front of him.

'What are you thinking? Come on, let's go,' he said staring at me. Now I should say something as we are going into a local place where if I was seen with him, it would mean that I was *dead*! My parents would kill me if they found out as they already didn't trust me, and if they saw or heard anything about me being with a guy, then it would be enough of a reason to kill me. Well, they wouldn't really kill me, but they probably would never talk to me again and, even worse, kick me out of the house.

'Don't worry, no one will see us, promise,' he said reassuring me. I looked at him and gave him a warm smile. 'OK, if you're sure.' And so we decided to go to the Starbucks Cafe, but separately by him walking in front, and me walking at the back. When we entered the cafe, he looked at me and pointed upstairs and straightaway I knew what he meant and went there. As I waited for Ares to come, my phone started to ring and guess who it was? Of course, it was him –Ares.

'Hey, do you like cappuccino?' he asked me. I absolutely loved cappuccino as that was the only thing I drank as it kept me awake.

'Yeah, I do, but don't buy anything please. I just want to talk to you,' I told him. As soon as I put the phone down, he was right in front of me. I didn't know what to say; I was just shocked.

'How did you get here so fast?' I asked him.

'Well, you said you wanted to talk to me, and so I came as soon as I could,' he said as he gave me a wink with his usual heart-warming smile. I just didn't know what to say; I mean this guy was so perfect. I just smiled at him and took a sip of my cappuccino. All of a sudden, he took my hand in his and started to stroke it gently. I could feel the warmth of his hand under mine, and my heart started to beat faster. It felt like my heart was beating for him only. And it felt like the world was spinning around me. Everyone in the coffee shop disappeared, and it felt like it was just me and him. What I was feeling was indescribable. I had never felt like that about anyone before. But then again, I had never been so close to a guy or had any sort of feelings either; so maybe what I felt was normal, right?

'So tell me, have you missed me?' I asked him softly. He just stared at me for a few seconds and finally answered me back, but not with words, with his eyes. At that moment, he got up and pulled his chair next to mine.

'Come on then, now I'm here. What did you want to talk about?' he said staring into my eyes. All my answers were given to me from the look of his eyes. I knew that if this wasn't love then it couldn't have been anything else. I just looked down staring into my cappuccino and at last I pushed myself to get some words out. Well, I did, but it sounded so much better in my head and it was really hard to explain what I wanted to say. It was only then that I realised how close he was sitting to me. I could feel his warm breath on my face and, all of a sudden, I tried to speak but no words came out. My voice unexpectedly felt tender; I could feel his face so close to my lips, and I just let my lips brush against his face and kissed him softly. His face was so soft. I didn't know what was happening; I just couldn't control myself, but then I realised what I wanted to say and that was it. I said everything in just one kiss. He got all his answers in just one kiss. He turned towards me and put his arm around my waist; I could feel his chest muscle go tight, and his hand slowly stroking my arm. I just started to feel dizzy and at the same time it felt the world was perfect. I had never before felt so happy and amazed in my life. It was a wonderful feeling. I felt like I was on top of the greatest mountain and the whole world was beneath my feet. If this was the feeling of love then I wanted it forever.

'Is this what you wanted to say?' he asked me as he lifted my chin up towards his face lightly.

'Yeah,' I said smiling, and he kissed me softly on my forehead.

'Excuse me, but we are closing in five minutes,' said the waitress standing in front of us, who we didn't even notice. As she walked off, I got up to go, but the truth was that I didn't want to go. I wanted to stay with Ares there—forever like that in his arms. I know it sounds stupid; obviously, you can't spend your life in a cafe, but you know what I mean. It was love. He started to stroke my face with back of his hand gently and whispered into my ear, 'I love you.'

I just wanted to kiss those soft lips of his so badly and now he made it even harder for me to control myself, but still I didn't kiss him. As I hugged him, I repeated the same words to him as well and walked off. A few steps away from him, I just stopped. I couldn't go any further, not without him. I turned around and started to run back towards him. I ran right into his arms. It felt like I was running into the doors of heaven. A sudden wind from the window hit my face and all my hair floated back. He held me tight in his arms. It felt like we were on top of the world.

'I don't want to go, Ares. I want to stay here with you. Forever . . . '

'Hey, hey, don't worry. You're not going to lose me. I'm yours forever, and I promise you that,' he said softly to me. Then he touched my soft hair and kissed me again on my forehead. To be honest, what he said kind of made me feel better, and I started to walk out of the cafe.

When I was finally out of the cafe, all I could think about was Ares and what had happened between us. However, the worst thing was that every time the thoughts came into my head, it made me cringe as I was feeling pleasure but also felt disgusted at the same time. But why? It was love, right? So this was what you were supposed to feel when you were in love? guilt? disgust? shame?

and happiness in equal measure? Because if this was the truth then I didn't want to be in love. I couldn't figure it out. What was happening to me?

*After Angel left, I was just shocked how close we had got. I couldn't figure out why she was always on my mind. I did have girlfriends before her but had never felt this way about them and the worse thing was I didn't see her as my girlfriend; she meant more to me. I felt responsible for her. I felt she was mine and that it was my duty to protect her and keep her away from harm. The girls that I had been with before, I didn't care about them. All it was for me was to have fun and, of course, it was the same for them. However, Angel was different; I had strange feelings for her. What did all this mean? Was this love? She meant my world. I knew that without Angel I wouldn't be complete.*

*'Excuse me, but we are closing now, so would you please make your way downstairs. Thank you,' said the waitress as she showed me the way out.*

*As I left the cafe, I thought to myself whatever was happening to me. I knew it was a good thing, and I was glad it was as I knew Angel was worth it.*

# Chapter 9

## Is It Love?

When I woke up in the morning, I felt like a new person as I was so happy. It was really weird because every little thing was making me smile and, trust me, I mean, every little thing, such as I was my smiling to myself as I was fixing bag for college. It was an amazing feeling, because when I usually woke up, I had a bad headache, and was far too scared to get out of my bed thinking someone would tell me off and other stupid things related to this.

'Someone's in really good mood this morning. I've never seen you this happy before. I wonder why?' Sonya said as she came into my room and gave me a little nudge.

'Let me guess, is it someone whose name beings with A?' she smirked. Although I was too happy to care, yet it was important to make sure no one heard her saying those things, especially the devil (Nikkie).

'Stop it, man! Someone might hear you, especially the devil. She's always around to get me in trouble,' I said to her smiling at the same time. I tell Sonya everything as you already know and, therefore, she constantly teased me.

'I still can't believe you came so close to him in such a short period of time,' shouted Kiran from the distance when she saw me walking towards the college gate.

'Why do you keep saying 'so close'? You make it sound like I've done something really dodgy; all we did was hug, and I don't understand what the big deal is. I mean, you jumped in the guy's lap when you only knew him for five minutes, remember?' I said to her.

'Yeah, but you're Angel, you're a good girl. I thought you're not into all this boyfriend/girlfriend stuff,' she said.

'I still stick to that, I'm not. I absolutely hate that kind of stuff, no offence to you all. But you don't understand, Kiran, this is different. It's very early to say this, but I can see my future in Ares's arms. I believe this is love, because I think when you fall in love, you should feel what I feel. It's indescribable, Kiran. We are not like you and your boyfriends that if we have an argument, we split up.'

'Hey! What you trying to say? Me and my boyfriends? I never had more than one boyfriend at a time!' she exclaimed.

'Come on, Kiran, man, you know what I mean,' I said as I hugged her.

'Yeah, Angel, you should already know her by now. Kiran is not like that. She only has two or three boyfriends at the same time,' Amar said laughing at the same time trying to run away from Kiran who was about to hit him.

'Stop it, you two, I know Kiran is not like that,' Sam yelled at us. But we both carried on laughing until we got to our lessons. We still had time, just then my phone started ringing and obviously I knew straightaway who it was as the people who usually phone me were already there with me. As I answered my phone, I walked away from them, and I knew Kiran would get me back since I had teased her so much earlier.

'Where are you going? Let me guess, is it your boyfriend again?' she yelled out from behind me. I laughed. 'He is not my boyfriend. He is my future be, OK. I'm not you, Kiran.' As I said that, I could hear Amar in background laughing at Kiran again.

At last, I spoke after having made the poor guy wait for so long. 'So I'm your future be? You didn't say future be what?' Ares said without even saying hello. I was so embarrassed as he shouldn't have heard that. Was I supposed to say that he was my future be fiancé, he would then think I was kind of rushing the relationship.

'I was just trying to get rid of Kiran as I hated the word "boyfriend", and you're my future be friend, OK,' I said laughing.

'OK, if that's how you see me,' Ares replied in kind of a down voice. I felt really bad; however, I couldn't say what he wanted to hear. It would've been far too soon for that kind of stuff.

As the days went by and seasons changed gradually, just like the seasons, my feelings for Ares kept getting stronger and stronger. I started becoming more dependent and more attached to Ares and spoke to him at least three times a day, and each time for a minimum of half an hour. All I knew at that point was that I had to talk to him every day, had to tell him all that I had done that particular day or what was bothering me, and the best thing was that he always made me feel better and told me that I would always have him. However, I still couldn't figure out what was happening to me, and why was I so attached to him? Once I even tried not to talk to him and wanted to see how I would feel, but I realised it was the most difficult thing I had ever done in my life. All I did was not talk to him for one day, and it felt like I had lost something so special and close to me as I was constantly searching around the house thinking it was somewhere around here. At the end of the day, I gave up and ended up calling him, and after that day, never tried it again; it was far too hard.

*What's happening to me? It's been three months since I saw my Angel. Wait, why am I saying 'my Angel'? Is she really mine? Why do I constantly think this amazing girl belongs to me? Since then I have been speaking to her continually (minimum three times a day) and I have realised my feelings have got stronger, and I think her feelings are the same too. I believe, she hasn't realised it yet like I have, but I know one thing, just like I cannot live without her, she too cannot live without me. And*

*I think it's time for me to tell her what we feel for each other as it really is love. However, not now, as it's getting close to her exams. I want her to do very well, and so I don't want to distract my Angel from her studies.*

After receiving my results, I realised that I needed to work much harder than that to impress my parents, especially my mum as I had achieved five Bs; well, it was good for someone who had been predicted Bs, but not for me as I was an A-grade student. I wasn't the only one shocked at my results, but my friends were too; I didn't know what to say to my parents or Ares. But most of them were close to A, so if I get As in summer, then my overall grade would definitely be As. Except that who was going to explain this to my parents; they wouldn't understand this. I just kept thinking positive, and told my parents what I had achieved, but they were pretty mad at me. But what could I do? However, I never told Ares as I knew he would be mad at me too, and I didn't want to ruin my Valentine's Day which was five days away. Yet he was different; he wasn't like before, and it felt like he had found out something bad about me. He phoned less, told me not to bother him too much, and when he did talk, it was as though I was imposing myself upon him. It just didn't make any sense, and when I asked my friends, they told me he was right and that I should give him some space. It was really confusing as they were always on my side and the worst thing was when I asked Sonya, she said exactly the same thing too. I know one thing that that Valentine's Day would suck. It was going to be absolutely terrible, and it was not fair, because I really thought it was going to be special. As for once, I had someone in my life.

Finally, the day came, and I had looked forward to the day with so much excitement. Well, I was excited but not any more; it felt like a normal day and the worse thing was that it was a Saturday. Meaning, I didn't have anything to do to keep my mind off that appalling day when everyone else was out having fun except me. To make the day even worse, Ares hadn't even bothered to send me at least one text to wish 'Happy Valentine's Day.'

'What are you doing lying there? Come on, get up.' Sonya came into my room and tried pulling me out of the bed.

'Why do I need to get up? It's not like anything special is happening. Please, Sonya, leave me alone. I just want this stupid day to go quickly,' I moaned.

'Listen!' she pulled my arm shouting at me, 'I'm not in a mood to baby talk and make you feel better. Do you understand? I'm pissed off as it is, so don't make my day worse. Wear these clothes, and I want to see you downstairs in half an hour,' and she walked out of my room. I didn't know what to say; I was just shocked at her behaviour as I had never seen her react like that. One thing I didn't understand was where did she want to go with me that early in the morning? I didn't even know what time it was and when I looked at my alarm clock, it said 12.05 p.m., oh my god! That's not early; I couldn't believe I had slept for that long. Maybe she wanted to take me out because she knew Ares had acted like an idiot in the past few days and that he hadn't done anything for me on V-Day. Yeah, I think that was it. I might as well get ready and have fun with my sweet younger sister who loved me so much. I really didn't know what I would do without her.

'Wow! You look really nice, Angel,' Sonya said really nicely as we left home.

'Well, you brought them for me, but one thing I don't understand is when did you go shopping without me and does Mum know we are going out?' I asked her.

'Angel, you ask too many questions. Can't we just enjoy this or you want to go back to bed and depress yourself? she replied cheekily. I guess she had a point. I definitely didn't want to go back to bed as it would have just made me madder at Ares.

'So where are we going? You have any plans,' I asked her.

'Angel, you talk too much, man. We just left home and since then you've been bombarding me with questions. Can't you just wait and see?' she said annoyed.

'No, I can't, you know how I'm and, anyway, who goes out at this time? It's far too early,' I answered her back.

'Well, tough, just wait and it's not early. Look at the time, it's 3.00 p.m. Just because you took six hours to get ready, it doesn't mean it's early,' she replied to me even more annoyed. She was right about the time, but she acted even more strangely when we got by the shopping centre entrance. She told me to go in and that she would go to the toilet from the other side of the shopping centre. It just didn't make any sense. Why does she need to go all the way round and not come the easy way with me? However, the shopping mall looked amazing from outside. I had never seen it that beautiful before and that was because they had never decorated it so romantic before. It was like entering the love world; there must be something special going on that day as they had made it that good. I started walking slowly towards the double door of the shopping centre as Sonya disappeared to the other side, and I pushed the doors open.

When it opened, I think I entered a dream world as what I saw was indescribable. All this was done for me or for someone else and my stupid sister was playing a practical joke on me, and if she was, then that was my worst nightmare. Everything was beyond my words; there were couples standing on both sides of the double doors all the way to the end of the mall, and the best thing was that all the ladies was wearing red dresses, and the gents was wearing black suits. When I looked at them, they all smiled at me and welcomed me in. As I started walking in, at the same time, I was searching for a familiar face such as my sister's, Ares's or Amar's, or any of them for that matter. When my eyes suddenly hit the ceiling, it was full of red heart lights hanging down, and the cutest thing was that inside all of them was my name written! I felt so much better and from seeing my name on all the balloons left me speechless—I knew that all that was really for me. As soon as I looked down, I saw Ares from the distance looking amazing and holding a rose of roses in this hand. I gave him a smile from where I was standing, and a few seconds later, I started running towards him. I just couldn't control myself. I needed to be close to him. As soon as I became close to him, I just stopped a few feet away from him. I didn't know what to say as he had left me speechless. I couldn't believe he had done all that for me! I stood there staring at him and, all of a sudden, he positioned himself in the way guys do when they are about to propose to a girl. I didn't know what to say or do. Was he going to ask me to marry him or something? However, instead of a ring, he looked into my eyes with his usually heart-warming smile and a rose in his hand. Finally, he gave me the rose and said softly, 'Would you be my valentine?' My eyes started watering with tears full of happiness, and, at last, I managed to say very quietly, 'Of course, I will.' I took the rose from his hand, still staring into his hazel-coloured eyes, and everyone around us started clapping. When I heard the clapping sound I remembered that the people were still there with us, and it wasn't just me and Ares. But one thing kept going round and round in my head and that was that all this was too good to be true. I still thought I was dreaming and that any minute then I was going to wake up. While I was talking to myself like always, I felt like I was flying, and when I looked down, I saw that Ares had picked me up. I started smiling at him, and then I gave him a blow kiss, and he started spinning me around. When I looked up, I could see that the light hearts on the ceiling were spinning too, and when I looked down, I saw Ares's face smiling at me.

If that was not a dream, then I was the luckiest girl in the world. I mean, how many girls have you seen who would have all this? I'll tell you the answer. There's none, *just me*! When he put me down, I just hugged him, because I wanted to be in his arms forever, even if it was a dream. I didn't want to wake up. That moment in his arms, I wanted to capture the moment forever.

I could see from the distance someone walking towards us; he looked familiar to me, but I couldn't remember where I had seen him. As he came closer, he did some strange handshake with Ares, and then looked at me with a smile.

'Hey, sis, you remember me?' he asked me. He was so sweet. He had seen me like his own sister, but I still couldn't remember him. Seriously, I couldn't; I knew I had seen him somewhere, but where?

'Come on, Angel, think,' he said.

Ooooohh yeah! I remembered him then. When I had first met Ares, he was there too. However, I never remembered him being that nice. He was wearing his black trouser with a red top which had the writing 'Tyson wants you,' and I wasn't sure what that meant.

'The name is Tyson,' he smiled.

'Nice to meet you.' I smiled back.

Ares took me to this romantic restaurant; basically, it was a love nest for lovebirds. That's how I would summarise it. It was a perfect place for couples on Valentine's Day, and the best thing was that there were a lot of other couples just like us. However, one thing kept irritating me, and I had to ask him that.

'How did you afford all this, Ares?'

'You don't like what I did for you? Is there anything missing?' he asked me.

I shook my head indicating a 'no'.

'Then don't worry about how I did this. You deserve this and much more and because I love you so much. OK?' he replied touching my hand. I gave him a smile and told him that I loved him too.

How he could afford all this was only a small part of the story, while the other part was that everyone I trusted was in it! I couldn't believe they actually managed to hide all this from me, even Kiran! I mean, she was one of those people who could never keep anything, not even for half an hour, forget days or even weeks. I knew from the past few weeks that they all had been acting strange, even Sonya, but I couldn't figure out why. All of a sudden, Ares woke me up from my second world. What was wrong with me? I always did this when something good happened to me. Couldn't I just shutdown my negative thoughts for a few minutes so that I could enjoy the good things which happened to me. I thought, 'OK, I'm going to do it now, no more thinking in my head, whatever comes I'm going to say it loud.'

'Are you OK?' Ares asked me in confusion after noticing my facial expressions.

I hate myself! Ooohhhh god! I'm doing it again, stop it, Angel!

'Yeah I'm fine. I'm still trying to get it in my head right. What you have done for me is amazing and because I still think I'm going to wake up from this amazing dream any minute.' I lied. I knew it wasn't a dream an hour ago, but what was I supposed to say? That I'm a freak, and I live in two worlds? He gave me a smile, meaning 'you deserve it,' which made me feel better as he had not figured out about my strange thoughts. Just as I was thinking that this could not get any better, all of sudden, he gave me a box which looked like a ring box. I didn't know what to say as I was so shocked at all the good things happening to me in one day. He took my hand and opened the box. Inside it was this breathtakingly beautiful ring and I cannot describe in words how beautiful it was. It was white gold with a huge, I mean *huge*, square-shaped gemstone; the colour was dark green, like emerald with lots of tiny diamonds dotted all around the gold. He left me speechless. As he put the ring on my right middle figure, I think I just froze for good couple of minutes or it could be even more as Ares was calling my name like ten times.

'Angel, are you OK?' I finally heard clearly.

'Yeah, I'm fine, sorry. I'm still getting my head round this,' I said still staring at the ring.

'Again?' he said in annoyance. 'Listen, Angel, I told you before, and I will tell you again, you're worth it all. Do you understand?'

I nodded my head indicating 'yes', and he continued, 'I still think you deserve even more as you have and are still going through so much in your life which you don't deserve. This is the least I could do for you. All I want is for my Angel to be happy, that's all.' I took his hands into mine, and all I wanted to say were three words; well, OK, not exactly three but eight.

'Did I tell you that I love you?' I asked smiling at him.

'Yeah, you did, but only once, so that doesn't count,' and we both laughed as he finished his sentence. All I could say was that that was the best day of my life, which I will never forget; well, except the morning.

'I can't believe you actually managed to hide all this from me,' I said to Sonya as we walked home.

'Well, you tell me, would it have been as fun and magical if I had told you about it?' she asked me. Now that I think about it, she was right; it would not have been this amazing, and the surprise made it extra special.

'Yeah, I guess you're right, and one thing, thank you. It means so much to me that I cannot describe how thankful I'm to you, all my best friends, and Ares, of course,' I told Sonya hugging her at the same time.

When we got home, everyone was in which was not good news as both of my parents hated me, as you already know, especially my mother. However, that night I did not care who hated or loved me as I had had an incredible day, and I was not going to let anything ruin it. As we came in, I ran straight into my room as I knew if I stayed downstairs, I would demolish my unforgettable day. I was a bit tired; however, it was far too early to go to sleep. It was only 6.30 p.m. So for like two hours, I sat there fixing my bag for college, doing some of my biology coursework, and my two math's homeworks. When I finished the last question of my mathematics homework, I started feeling a bit hungry. However, I did not want to go downstairs because everything had been perfect since I came home, and I did not want to mess it up by going downstairs.

By the time I came back upstairs, I was so tired that I did not care what time it was. I just wanted to sleep. Everyone else was asleep even before I went to eat so that was good for me. I got into my bed, did my prayer, and thanked God for that wonderful and unforgettable day. Before I closed my eyes, I wished that everything that had happened that day (except the morning) would all come in my dreams. Not just on that particular night but every night. That day was an unforgettable chapter in my life—one which would last forever in my dreams.

# Chapter 10

## Family's Blood

It was Monday morning, and I couldn't wait to see my friends. I wanted to thank them for what they had done for me. There was this saying that in your worst times the only people you will have that will be there for you will be your family. But I totally disagree with this as I never had my family (except Sonya); I always had my two . . . well, now, three best friends.

As soon as I got out of the car, waited for Dad to go then I ran towards the college gates where they all always waited for me, and I hugged all three of them at the same time. The first thing I shouted out, 'I love you all so much! I can't believe you all did that for me, but I hate you all at the same time too.'

'I don't understand which one is it? Love or hate?' Amar smiled looking at Sam.

'Both, well, I love you all more, because you did all that for me, but I hate you all too as you hid it all from me,' I answered back.

'Come on, man, forget all the hate. You know you enjoyed it, especially at the end,' Kiran pointed towards my hand with the ring in it. I couldn't say she was wrong. She was 200 per cent right, and I think I had said those words in my head a hundred times 'the best day of my life!'

It was finally official that we were in love; it felt odd to use the word 'love' as I had never been in love before. I mean, for other teenagers my age it was normal to say as they had lots of boyfriends, e.g. Kiran, but I don't think it was actually love, because if it had been, then they wouldn't break up after few weeks or months. It was unbelievable how much time we spent talking on the phone; everyone was telling us we spent more time on the phone than sleeping or revising, but I didn't think that. We only spoke for like one or two hours about four or five times a day. I didn't think that's too much; well, if you add the hours, it does sound too much. But we were happy. The sweetest thing about talking to or texting Ares was that at the end, he always told me that he loved me, which made me feel so special as no one in my life had actually acted like that towards me. However, the strangest thing was that when he was so nice to me, my parents' anger didn't bother me at all. Previously, I used to cry and ask God why was this happening to me, but now it didn't bother me as I knew I had someone in my life who couldn't take a step without me.

Anyway, we talked a lot, but we saw each other only once a month as too much wasn't good. We both had studies to do, anyway. But it wasn't like we did anything sexual, apart from the kissing. I believed in sex after marriage and no matter how hard it would have been for me, I knew I wouldn't change my mind on my morals. Every time we saw each other, all we did was talk or go out for a meal or watch a movie, and that was it—apart from the odd kiss which we gave each other on the cheeks. Our intention was to get to know each other and see if we could spend our future together.

However, one thing I completely forget about was my phone bill. I had phoned Ares so many times that I didn't even realise that my contract was on Mum's name. If she saw the bills, I would be dead as you can't image how many times I had phoned him in one day; it was like thirty or forty times. But you know sometimes when you phone someone, and it goes straight to answer phone because of no network connection, then the number of seconds doesn't get displayed. If my parents happen to see that then they'll not see how many seconds I had spoken, but they would just see how many times I had dialled a particular number. One thing I was most terrified of was the phone bills coming through the post, and then I knew my parents would kick me out of the house. I really needed to do something before I got into trouble and for my parents to hate me even more than they already did then. I then decided to change the bills to online instead of them coming through the post. That way only I could see the bills and no one else. I still had bad days like before, but one thing was different for sure and it was Ares. Now I had someone who cared about me and whatever problems I had he was there to help me and tell me that everything would be OK as long as I had him.

When it hit August, I was absolutely panicking as August meant *results*! I still remember 28 August last year as it was one of the worst days of my life as my mum wasn't happy with my grades, and I still couldn't figure out why. My grades were much better than most people's. It was even worse now as my A levels were ten times harder than GSCE, and I was sure I was definitely not going to get an A in stupid biology. As 24 August got closer, I felt like the few last days of my being alive were reaching their end. But Ares, Sonya, and my friends all kept telling me that I would do well and that I shouldn't panic so much as at the end of the day it were only exam results and not end of the world. That night I went to sleep praying I had done well; I didn't exactly sleep, but I was just in bed with my negative thoughts.

I think everyone had noticed how petrified I was when I got to college to collect my results, even though I acted strong. I really didn't understand why I was scared; I really did felt like my life depended on my results, however, 90 per cent was because of my parents. They wanted me to do so well that I didn't care any more about what I wanted. All I cared about was what they wanted and what made them happy, that's it. When I finally got the brown envelope, my hands were literally shaking, and I looked like I was having a panic attack. My whole body felt like it was about to shut down. Constant sweat was dribbling down my palms. Amar noticed me first and shouted towards me, 'Angel, are you OK? Look at me, stop this craziness, you're going to go crazy. For God's sake, it's only stupid exam results, and it's not worth this entire thing. Do you understand me?'

I stared at him for couple of seconds looking confused like I had never seen him in my life before and, all of a sudden, all my memory came back. Then I realised where I was and what was happening to me.

'Angel, do you want me to open your results for you?' Kiran asked me really calmly making sure not to scare me. I nodded my head slowly to her indicating a yes, but deep down, I felt like I was about to throw up. As she started opening the envelope, the sound of it was so loud to my ears that I couldn't hear anything else around me but the opening of the envelope. 'Crunch . . . Crackle . . . C-crackk . . .,' the sound of the opening of the envelope echoed into my brain. It was like a drum being banged on louder and louder.

'What the hell is wrong with you, Angel?' shouted Kiran when she looked at my results slip.

'Kiran, we are trying to make her feel better not to send her to hospital, you're not bloody helping by shouting like that,' Amar whispered to her at the same time pinching her. Kiran continued with her loud mouth.

'What? I'm serious. She was almost having an heart attack over nothing. Look at these grades! They are ten times better than mine.' When I heard those words from her mouth, my face started to lighten up a bit, and I started getting some colour in my cheeks. I could feel it.

'Really, Kiran? You're not joking with me, are you?' I said to her with a massive smile on my face.

'You don't believe me? Look at it yourself, man.' She gave the results slip to me. Surprisingly, she was right. I did do well, but I knew it wasn't good enough for my parents as I had achieved AABBB in my first year of A levels. I looked at Amar as he knew how my parents were like, especially my mum and now I was too scared to go home, because I didn't want the scene which had taken place last year to be repeated. But Amar reassured me that they would understand as I had tried my best. Moreover, A levels were hundred times tougher than GCSEs.

I started walking home, and I prayed to Allah (God) that hopefully Amar was right. I also phoned Ares on my way home and told him the results I had achieved. He was very sweet and understanding. He told me that I had done well and next time I should work even harder and push all my grades to As. But I never knew all that joy was only going to last for twenty minutes, and it would all change as soon as I entered the house. Well, guess what? I was right. Cos as soon as I announced my results to my parents, my mum stared at me for a few seconds and turned to my dad and said, 'Didn't I tell you she will do worse than her GCSEs, and you know the reason too?' What on earth was she talking about? What was the bloody reason? I was so sick of those stupid secrets about me that I didn't even know about. I had to know what the secret was about and who had spread such nonsense about me.

'What's the reason? What have I done that I don't know about,' I asked really politely so she wouldn't shout at me.

She looked at me and then started shouting, 'If you had spent less time having boyfriends and giving this family a bad name, then you would have done well. But it's too late now. Once a Muslim girl turns to that kind of stuff, it's very difficult to bring her back.' I just stared at her for good few minutes completely confused, thinking what the hell she was talking about. For God's sake, how could I do well if my parents, especially my mum were constantly saying that I gave them a bad name and that they wished they never had me? How could you study when every minute of your life was spent in constant argument, in being hurt, and in hearing things from your mother that you would never expect? But I never voiced my feelings to them as I knew there was no point; they would never listen. I walked out of the living room and went straight into my room, because I really didn't have any more space in my brain for anything else, and especially not about how terrible a daughter I was as that was one thing I wasn't. I could give my life up for my father's name. But if loving someone was wrong then I didn't know what was right.

When I entered my room, the first thing I saw was my reflection in the mirror, and then I realised I was so into making my parents proud that I had completely forgotten about Angel; to me Angel didn't even exist any more. I was just a doll to impress my parents. I had truly lost myself; I didn't know who I was any more as I didn't care about myself. That's why I got hurt very easily as I tried so hard to keep them happy, but I never succeeded in it. I wiped my tears away and phoned Ares as I needed to talk to someone, because if I didn't, I would go crazy. All this was too much for me to handle! My reflection in the mirror was disturbing. I looked pale with black patches under my eyes. As soon as Ares picked up and before I could say anything, I burst out into tears, and Ares knew straightaway that it was because of my stupid results.

'Stop it, Angel, right now,' he yelled down the phone. 'I don't want to see you in tears any more. Your eyes are not worth tears, you're my Angel. You have angel eyes, and they are not made for that. What's wrong with you? Why do waste your time and get yourself hurt like this? I can't stand it. Listen to me, Angel, you're mine now, and they got no right to hurt my Angel. So, whatever they say, just ignore it as you're only going to be there for a maximum of another three to four years, and then you will be with me. OK, *Jaan*? So stop crying, and anyway only I've got the right to hurt you, no one else,' he joked at the end.

'Hey!' I yelled out laughing at the same time at his joke, 'What do you mean only you can hurt me? If that's the case, then I can hurt you too.'

'Don't worry, no one else hurts me anyway besides you,' he said laughing over the phone. I had this habit that Ares called the 'the cry thing' when he saw or heard me doing the fake cry, and then he knew straightaway that I was annoyed about something he did or said. Therefore, now I did that, and he quickly said, 'I'm joking, babes. You know how much I love you.'

'Ares, what am I going to do without you?' I asked him just to see what he would say and surprisingly he said, 'Nothing, you will live your life very happily.' I then got so mad at him. How could he say that so easily?

'Ares, come on tell me,' I said moaning.

'OK, fine. You will do nothing, only one thing will happen . . .' he took a long pause, 'that you will die,' he said. Ares was completely right; without him I would die as he was the one who had given me this wonderful new life, and for once in my life, I had got someone who cared so much about me and could not see a second of his life without me. Just to have someone like that felt absolutely amazing. When I put the phone down, for a few minutes, I tried to imagine my life without Ares, and it sounded and looked so scary that it was far too horrible to describe. My world without Ares was just simple one colour . . . one odd colour . . . just white.

All of a sudden, I realised how quiet the house was. I mean, in the two hours I had been in my room, no one had come in to disturb me, and even Sonya hadn't come in either to check on me like she always did. It was strange, and I wanted to know what was going on and where was everyone? I ran downstairs and asked one of the maids where everyone was, and I was right. There was no one was home. However, I wished I hadn't asked as what I found out wasn't nice or fair. It hurt me a lot.

What had happened was that one of Dad's close friends had invited us to his house like a month ago, and when I found out, I was so excited to go, but now they all had gone without me. None of them had even bothered to ask me if I wanted to go or not. I couldn't believe they had done that, and I felt like I was a ghost floating around. A lost soul! It was at that point I wished I hadn't asked where they had gone.

I phoned Ares again and told him everything, but instead of comforting me, he said, 'So what, let them go, but tell me this, what time are they coming back?'

I couldn't believe him. Did he call this comfort? 'Well, I got news for you, Ares. This is not comfort, OK!' I thought.

'I don't know, probably late as they went an hour ago I think, but why do you want to know, anyway?' I asked him.

'Well, it's only 1.00 p.m., and they are not coming back till late, so do want to go out with me?' he asked me.

'Yeah, I do want to go out, but . . .' I took a long pause. Of course, I wanted to go out with him; everyone was out having their fun, and I was stuck at home depressed, even though I was the one who had done well. And, besides, I should've been the one celebrating as I had got my results, and they were really good. However, I felt like I wasn't alone in my room and that someone else was there with me, and when I looked up, it was the maid. I started panicking as she might have heard me saying Ares's name, but she came in and sat next to me.

'Say yes to your friends, you deserve a day out, Angel. You have done very well in your first year. Come on, get ready quickly and come back before your parents come home, because I don't want you to get in trouble. OK?' she said smiling fondly at me. 'If you were my daughter, I would love you more than anything in this world, and let me tell you something, Angel,' she said as she sat down beside me on my bed. 'In life, sometimes, we just have to accept things like these, you're truly an angel. I see you like my daughter, and if you ever want to talk then I am here to listen.' She gave me a hug and wiped my tears away.

'Christiana, thank you,' I said.

'Don't thank me,' she said walking out my room. I loved all the staff in my house. All of them were so nice and caring towards me that it was unbelievable. I think they all knew that it wasn't my fault and all those arguments that had happened in our house, weren't also my fault. I gave her a hug and quickly got ready. I told Ares to meet me in the restaurant at the shopping centre where we usually ate, and the best thing about that place was that it was in a corner so it wasn't a chaotic place. All I could say was that I loved him too much as he had made my day perfect again like always, and I completely forgot how bad my morning had been. It was all thanks to Ares.

Most girls say 'we prefer our guy to take us to expensive places, to buy us expensive gifts like diamond rings,' but I . . . I didn't want any of that as I had all of it, and I can tell you one thing no material possession can keep you happy. All I wanted was basically my Ares—the perfect guy in this world—for me, anyway. I just wanted to have a laugh for a couple of hours and completely forgot all the problems I had, just like today's problems. We ate in the restaurant where we met, then we went for a walk in the park, and we lay down on the grass for good couple of hours.

'Ares, can I ask you something?' I said lying on his chest.

'Yeah, sure you can, Angel, anything you want,' he said, while playing with my hair. I got up and looked into his eyes. 'Ares, do you ever think about the future?'

He paused for a few seconds, and then touched my left cheek. 'Yeah, I do, always.'

'What do you see?' I asked, still looking into his eyes.

'What do you see?'

'Ares, I'm serious, what do you see?'

He got up completely, held both my hands, and slowly whispered . . . 'Angel, I see you.'

His warm breath gently touched my face.

'I love you, Ares,' I said quietly.

'I do too, but more.' He winked.

It was such a nice day that I completely forgot about not having gone to my dad's friend's house, and I managed to come home before my parents had.

I was in the dining room having my dinner when Dad came in. I just wanted to act normal and completely forget about the scene that had taken place that morning.

'How is your friend and his family?' I asked Dad. He stared at me for a few seconds thinking how I knew where they had been to.

'It was good, and they kept asking about you and why you hadn't come, and one of his sons is the same age as you, Angel, but he did really badly in his A levels.' He kept telling me that you should have come and helped his son out. 'But, Angel, I just want to say that I know I have been very harsh on you, however, that doesn't mean I'm not . . .' before he could finish off his sentence, my mum interrupted him by saying, 'She was too busy with her boyfriend to go with us.' I thought, 'She keeps saying boyfriend, and she doesn't even know about Ares. What would happen if she did know about him?' It really scared me when I thought about it, but I was not going to ruin my day because of Mum's words.

That night I had such a horrible dream that it didn't make sense at all to me. In my dream, I was running in this dark pathway, but I never reached my destination, and it just kept going and going, and whatever I had in my pockets, like valuable things, I kept losing them. It was a very weird dream, but thank God it was just a dream; however, one thing kept bothering me that day which was that why was I losing things in my dream? I just couldn't figure out what it meant. Not only that I had a weird dream, but also Mum was a completely different person that week. I know you're probably thinking that she was much nicer to me. Well, you're wrong. She became ten times worse than how she was before. That week was absolutely a horrifying week, it really was. The worse thing was that I didn't have college, now that summer holidays had started and so I was at home all the time with Mum cursing me. I couldn't wait for that stupid week to be over as I didn't have a clue as to what I had done wrong that she hated me more than before. Well, my week was good till 6.00 p.m., because everyone was then out of the house, and I just relaxed; however, after 6.00 p.m., I went straight to my room till the next day as I knew if I had stayed downstairs, then Mum would get pissed off just by the sight of me.

The next morning, I woke up at around 11.00 a.m. like all other days; I came downstairs singing after my shower and went straight into the dining room for my breakfast. As soon I entered, my voice just got cut off. It wasn't nice cut off like I forgot the song but it just shock cut off. In the dining room, both my parents were waiting for me; it really did feel like that because otherwise why would they both be home and not at work. They just sat and stared at me as I was standing by the door. I walked towards the dining room table and sat down where my breakfast was and really joyfully I asked Dad, 'How come you didn't go to work today?'

'Who is this guy and what have you done with him? Tell us everything truthfully, no more lies.' Mum looked straight into my eyes, and I could feel her anger. Suddenly, I froze still. I knew straightaway that they had found out about Ares, but how and who had told them? I thought to go for the safe option and deny everything.

'W-h-a-t guy, Mum? I don't know what you are talking about.'

'Really? Are sure you? Well, maybe, these will jog your memory,' she yelled and at the same time threw a bunch of papers on my face. I looked down towards the papers all over the table and realised they were phone bills. But not any phone bill, my phone bills with Ares's number on every page! My eyes just popped out of my head with tears coming down my face as now I was 100 per cent sure they had found out about Ares.

'Mum, there is nothing going, he's just a friend from college, that's it,' I whispered crying as my voice just shook.

'Don't lie to me! All this time I treated you bad. However, I always told myself that you will never do something that would actually give the family a bad name. But now I've realised I was wrong,' she yelled to my face. 'Angel, I'm asking you for the last time. Tell me who he is and what is going on between the two of you?' she screamed even louder.

All through my mind, my head was spinning and, for a moment, everyone stood still but me. Everything blackened out but the bills on the table. Ares's numbers were all sticking out. I took a deep breath. 'There is nothing going. He's just a friend,' I lied again, at the same time, crying. I knew it was pointless by keeping on repeating myself to Mum as she would never believe me, so I turned to my dad and whispered, 'Dad . . .,' but before I could say anything else, I felt my left eye completely lose its vision for a few seconds and my face in pain. I put my hand over the side of my face where Dad had slapped me and just looked down. I knew then that I had lost my family forever. I couldn't believe all this happened in a split second, and the worst thing was that I had lost the trust of my dad.

'Don't you dare say a word, Angel? It's too late now, just please get out of my face,' Dad said calmly. I started walking towards the door and at the same time tears rolled down my face and behind me Mum yelled out again.

'Don't think this is it, I will find your boyfriend. You will get married to him and you will leave my house, because I don't want poison like you in this house to ruin my other two daughters' lives.' It's indescribable how much her words hurt; I really did wish she rather hit me than say those words because the pain of her hitting me would always go away, but the pain of her words would never leave my heart. Before I walked out the room, I turned to see my dad's face. Fatedly, I saw a tear drop from his eyes, then suddenly . . . b-b-b-break . . . my heart shattered into millions of pieces. I felt like my heart would pop out of me any minute then. I went straight to my room and continued crying in my bed as I was so confused and lost. I really didn't know what to do. Even worse was that my mum had my phone and I was absolutely terrified that Ares might phone, and then I would be in huge trouble. But what terrified me the most was he might get into deeper trouble than me.

The following day when I woke up, I had a terrible headache; it was so painful that it felt like my head was about to explode. I sat up and noticed Sonya sitting on my bed with a tray of food on my table. I knew she had found out about everything as there was so much pain on her face that even when she tried to fake it with a smile, I could see right through it.

'Come on, eat your food before it gets cold,' she said and we both broke down crying.

'I really don't understand how all this happened, Sonya. It was all so quick and so sudden that I didn't even have time to think. I'm so confused, Sonya, and so hurt. I don't know what to do. Please help me. What should I do? I'm so hurt, I have lost control of my life,' I said crying.

'OK, first you need to text him from my phone and tell him not to phone or text on your number as there were few private number missed calls on your phone. I know you're going to ask me how I know. I heard Mum telling Dad, and after that you need to eat, because I know you haven't eaten all day,' she replied back wiping her tears. After she had finished off telling me what to do, I straightaway texted Ares and told him that I would explain everything the next day. Then I asked her one thing which was how to go on from there.

'But, Sonya, what do I do now? I mean, do I carry on talking to him or stop? But I don't know if I can stop talking to him, because now my life is hundred times worse than before, and I cannot be without Ares at the worst times of my life. I need him, Sonya,' I cried even more.

'Listen to me, Angel, you're my elder sister. I'm sure you know what the best thing for you is. However, I don't want to lose you from my life. You mean too much to me. So if you still want to be in this house, then please take my advice and forget about him. I know it's going to hurt, and I know it's going to be difficult, but you have to, Angel, but again I'm going to leave it up to you.' She hugged me. 'Life without Ares . . . I'm going to die,' I thought. But Sonya was right. I had to do this.

The next morning, I phoned Ares from Sonya's phone as she had left it at home for me and I told Ares to meet me at that restaurant place where we usually met. However, Mum had told all the staff not to let me out of the house, but she didn't know one thing which was that all the staff loved me. I told the maid that I was doing this to bring peace into my house, so she should please let me go.

When I got to the restaurant, he was already there waiting for me. As soon as I saw him, I just burst out into tears and ran into his arms.

'Hey, hey, don't do that please. You said we were going to talk, but if you're going to cry, then I'm going back,' he said softly to me and kissed me on my forehead like always. I told him everything that had happened, but I couldn't tell him about what Sonya had said at the end.

'Angel, didn't I tell you that you're really bad at hiding things from me?' he said to me.

'Hiding? I'm not hiding anything. Honestly, all this really happened,' I told him.

'No, I'm not saying you're lying. I'm saying you didn't finish off what you wanted to say, and there is something else you want to tell me as well,' he said.

'OK, fine if you really want to know, then I'll tell you. Well, Sonya said that if I wanted to stay in the house and not to lose my family, then I should stop contacting you. But that's not going to happen, no way, Ares. I can't do that I'm sorry,' I told him. He didn't say anything; he just turned his head towards the window and stared for a couple of minutes before turning back towards me.

'I think your sister is right,' he finally answered with tears coming down his face. I just stared at him in shock for a few seconds, and my eyes started to fill with tears.

'Are you crazy? Do you know what you're saying? No, no way, I can't do this, Ares. I'm sorry,' I yelled out and at the same time I ran out of the restaurant. He came running after me and pulled me towards himself.

'Listen, Angel, we have to do this, and there is no other way. Your sister is right. If you don't, then you will lose them forever, and I know you don't want that.'

'But what about us? What am I going to do without you? I will go crazy, and you know that.' I started to pull his collar.

'I'm not saying this is it, of course, we will be together. You're mine and no one will take you away from me, but just not now. Go finish your college, go to university, and then we will see, because then I will be here and you will here for each other. However, your family wouldn't be if you lose them now. So please, Angel, try to understand me. I love you so much and promise you no one will take your place. I got something to give you which will definitely assure you that you're mine and only mine.' At the end his voice started to shake. He took a box out of his pocket which looked like a ring box and when he opened it, there was this beautiful engagement ring inside it. It was absolutely breathtaking; he took it out of the box and placed it on my figure.

'Now you're mine and this should reassure you that I will never be without you,' he said with tears coming down his face. I couldn't believe this was really happening. I had never imagined my life without Ares. It was too horrible to imagine and now it was really happening. I knew that true love could never last forever. If Romeo and Juliet didn't end up together, then there was no chance for us.

'I s-h-oul-d . . . go now.' I tried to take the words out of my mouth.

'Since it's our last time, can I give you a lift?' he asked me. I was so hurt that I couldn't talk any more, but I managed to shake my head indicating yes. I put my head on his shoulder, and he put his arms around me, and we started walking towards his car. I still couldn't believe this was really happening. I'm going to be without my Ares, and I don't think I could do that. As he started driving, he kept telling me that I should never disappoint my parents and do whatever that kept them happy because he was not going to be there to tell me all that stuff again. My throat kept filling up with tears. Then suddenly all the tears started to roll down my cheeks. My heart shattered to pieces again. My whole world just crashed onto me. I was completely hopeless.

A few houses away, he stopped the car and told me that I should always be good and listen to whatever my parents said. I didn't say anything but just shook my head like before. As tears continued coming down my face, he wiped them away.

'I love you so much that it's indescribable and that ring you're wearing is a sign of our future. We will be together, Angel. I promise this to you.' He hugged me for the last time and then kissed me on my forehead. As I turned to open the car door, I noticed a car next to Ares's looking very similar to my dad's car. As I continued staring out the tinted window to see who it was that was inside the car, I realised it wasn't a similar car to my dad's . . . it was my dad's car! And the figure that came out of the car was my dad! As my dad came out of the car, I just froze. I couldn't do anything, but I knew one thing that my life would change forever after that very day. He dragged me out of Ares's car and told me to go and sit in his car. When I tried to tell him what was going on, he told me to shut up and get in the car. As I got in his car, he stared at Ares for a few seconds and came back to his car. I tried so hard to explain everything to him, but the first thing he said was, 'Enough! I've heard and have seen enough. I don't want to hear anything else from you. I can't even look at you, because I don't know who you are any more.' After he had said that, I just went quiet. I didn't know what was wrong with me, for even when I tried to make things better, they became ten times worse. I really didn't know what to do any more.

'Please, just listen to me. I haven't done anything. You're taking it all the wrong way, please, Mum . . . Dad you have to believe me.' Warm tears fell from my eyes as my hand gripped onto my Hello Kitty bag.

'Get out, Angel! I'm ashamed to even have named you as Angel. You bring disgrace to the name itself. I named you Angel because they meant to be clean—clean from heart and soul and today you proved me wrong, very wrong, and you put shame to the name and to my legacy! Get out my house!' My dad's voice was like a jab in the ribs. My heartbeat was fast . . . then it got faster, and then at its fastest point. I could feel warm blood shooting through my veins. From where I was standing, it looked like a horror movie set—closed up and quiet—too quiet.

I knew there was no point in explaining anything any more as they weren't prepared to listen, and the only choice I had was to leave home because that was the only thing that would make them happy.

As I walked down the stairs with my bag in my hand, it felt like I was taking the last few steps towards my death as I knew I would never come back to that house again and that was it. When I got by the door, I saw Sonya in tears with Sameer next to her asking why she was crying and Dad close to them trying to control his emotions. But the worst feeling for any young girl can be to see her mother standing on the other side of the corridor and not caring about her daughter or where she would end up. I don't ever wish this to happen to anyone as the pain in your heart would be too much to handle, especially when you know you haven't done anything. I didn't say anything, just wiped my tears away and started walking towards the door.

As I opened the door to leave, all of a sudden, Sonya came running towards me, hugged me, and started screaming, 'Please, Angel don't go, what am I going to do without you? This house is nothing without you. You're the one who brings all the fun and laughter to this house. Please don't go, Sis, please.' She continued crying and my heart just broke into a million pieces. She was right. What was I going to do without her?

'Mum . . . Dad, please don't kick her out. I will be good. I will do my homework . . . anything, just don't let her go, please.' Sonya grabbed my dad's foot. At least, Sonya had Dad, but who did I have? No one. All I wanted to do right then was to hug her and tell her that I was not going anywhere and was staying there with her. But I couldn't as I knew it would never happen. I had lost that chance.

'Look at me, Sonya, what you saying is not correct. OK? Your job is here to keep Mum and Dad happy. Do you understand me?' I yelled to her, and she nodded her head indicating a yes.

'This is something I couldn't do, but I know you will definitely achieve it. Be good always, OK?' I finished off. From where I was standing, I looked at Dad, and I could see tears rolling down his small round eyes, but I tried to control my emotions, so I didn't hurt him any more. I walked towards Dad and straightaway hugged him and asked him, 'Is there anything you want me to do

Dad when I'm not here?' I said with a broken voice. He looked at me and finally replied, 'Just promise me you're going to stick to your name.'

'Of course, I will, Dad. I always have, and I promise you that the day will come when you will find out I am innocent and that I haven't done anything wrong to put our family's name to shame.'

'Angel, where are you going?' Sameer asked me pulling my jeans. I bent down to get to his height and told him, 'Don't worry, I promise I will be back soon, and you know how much I love you.'

Then I turned to Mum and when I was about to say something, she turned her face away from me, and Nikkie standing next to her did the same thing. I had to say what I wanted to say before I went, 'Now that I'm leaving your life forever, can you please do one thing, Mum and forgive me? Please, I'm sorry for anything I have done to hurt you, and one more thing, Mum, keep yourself happy always. I love you, Mum, always.' I just stared at her, then at Nikkie, and then at the photograph of our whole family on our living room wall.

I opened the door. Amar and Kiran were standing there for me, and when I was about to leave, something grabbed my hand. I turned around to see what it was, and it was Sameer. He was in tears and started yelling, 'Don't go, Angel. I know you're not coming back. Who is going to read me bedtime stories when you're gone or watch my video with me? Please don't go.'

Sameer's tears destroyed me from the inside out. I couldn't control myself any more, and I burst out crying and hugged him. At the same time, I looked at Sonya giving her a sign to take him away from there. Amar took my bag, and I put my head on Kiran's shoulder and walked out of the house crying. I turned around and looked back at my family for the last time as I knew I would never see them again. That was it! Because of a stranger's love, I had lost my family's blood.

Only when I got away from the house did I realise where I was going to go. I had never thought about that! I turned to Kiran, and the first thing I said to her was, 'I need to see Ares now.' She looked at me in disbelief. 'What the hell is wrong with you? Because of that idiot you lost your family and now you want to see him? Are you feeling OK?' I didn't reply to her as I didn't know what to say, but I was 100 per cent sure that all that happened was not his fault. To keep my family's *izzat* (honour) he had told me to do whatever it was that kept them happy, and he had also stopped all kind of contact he had with me. But I don't blame Kiran as she didn't know anything, and even if I told her, she would never believe me due to her own experiences. As Amar started driving, I asked Kiran again to phone Ares, and this time she didn't say anything and just did it.

*I had never felt this horrible before; it felt like something bad was going to happen or had happened either to me or my Angel. I didn't really care about myself; however, I didn't want anything to happen to her as she didn't have anyone to tell her that everything would be OK. I was so used to talking to her that like a kid I kept staring at my phone thinking any minute then she was going to phone me. I knew that was not going to happen, but for some reason, I had hope that it would ring and her number would just pop up. I know it sounds really stupid. I took my phone out of my pocket and started staring at her photo which was my wallpaper and remembered the day when I had taken that photo. As I was staring, my phone started ringing. I got so happy that my Angel had phoned me, but when I read the name, it said Kiran. Why was she phoning me? She never phoned me; the only time she did was when she wanted to complain about how bad I was to Angel. Anyway, when I answered, the first thing she said to me was,*

*'Angel wants to see you now. I don't know why, but I think she's going crazy because a normal person wouldn't want to see you.'*

*I didn't know what to say, so I immediately put the phone down on her, and when I turned round I saw Tyson standing behind me.*

*'Let me guess, was that my sister?' he asked me.*

*'No, it was her friend, Kiran. She said Angel wanted to see me right now, but I'm not going to go.'*

*'No, Ares, you are going to go because this is the last time she's going to see you, so go and see what she has got to say,' Tyson told me.*

*My phone started to ring again, and it was Kiran again. I picked up and told her I would be there in twenty minutes.*

When I got out of the car, Amar grabbed my hand and said, 'You're not going alone. We are coming with you.' I knew if I said no, they wouldn't have let me go, so I gave them a smile indicating yes. When I saw Ares from a distance waiting for me, I told Amar and Kiran to wait where they were standing as I wanted to talk to him alone. It was a very strange day as it being the hottest month (August) the weather was so cloudy that even when it was only 3.00 or 4.00 p.m., it looked like it was 7.00 or 8.00 p.m. My heart told me that seeing Ares was going to turn out to be dark cloud.

As soon as I saw it was him, I just ran towards him crying. When I was finally in his arms, I felt as though everything was perfect just like before, and I just wanted to be in his arms forever as I had realised that the only place I could get peace was in his arms. All of a sudden, he pulled me away from himself, stared into my eyes for a few seconds in which I could see a lot of pain just like in mine, and he asked, 'What's the problem that you wanted to see me so urgently?' I didn't know where to start and wanted to say to him, 'I'm just totally lost.' But I had to tell him everything as he was my last hope.

'You know how my dad saw us . . .,' but before I could finish off, he interrupted, 'I know he must have been mad at you at home, but Angel you promised me that you were going to do this. Remember, you said it yourself, no more seeing or talking? They will be mad at you for a few days, then after that, they will be fine. OK?'

'Yes, I know. I remember saying that, but the problem is that . . .,' again before I could finish off, he interrupted me; however, this time he yelled at me, 'Don't you get I don't want to be with you? Stop bothering me so much and go back home. I'm sick of you. You're my biggest mistake which I regret in my life. Now just leave me alone and get lost!'

Tears started flowing down my eyes, and I froze where I was standing. I didn't know what to do any more. One thing I knew was that I had lost everything

I had in my life for a stranger's love and now I realised I had made the biggest mistake of my life. Rain started pouring down, and I could see Ares disappearing in the distance. Each rain drop hitting my face felt like acid burning, because I didn't want to live any more. I had nothing left in this cruel world. I just fell to the ground and started yelling towards the sky, 'Why Allah? Why is this happening to me? What wrong have I done in my life to deserve this?'

Kiran and Amar ran towards me; they both sat next to me with Kiran hugging me. With every step Ares took away from me, it felt like a piece of my heart was breaking even more. A stranger's love and family's blood . . . I had lost both of it. The rain got stronger and stronger and not once did Ares turn to face me. He was gone, and with him he took my broken heart too.

'Ooooohh sweetie, don't cry. Please don't, babes. You haven't done anything bad to deserve this. You will be OK, because you will always have us always,' Kiran said hugging me and was in tears just like me.

'I was going to go after him and beat the shit out of him, but Kiran didn't let me. She said it was for your own good that he was out of your life.' Amar said in really pissed off way. Even when I looked up at him, I saw tears in his eyes too.

*As soon as I got round the corner where Tyson was waiting for me, I just broke down as I couldn't believe I had actually said all that stuff to the love of my life. The girl that I could not imagine my life without! How could I do this to her? Tyson sat next to me.*

*'Listen to me very carefully, Ares. We both know that I love her just like my own sister, and a brother can never see her little sister in pain, but if it's for her own good, then we have to do this for her. OK?'*

*He was right, but I never knew it would be so hard and painful. I looked round the corner to see if my Angel was still there, but I wish I hadn't looked back, because she was on the ground crying in pain. For every tear that dropped from her eyes, my heart started to shatter. I had done this to her. How could I be so cruel then? Now I couldn't do this any more. It was far too painful; I had to go to her. She needed me, and I needed her more than ever. I stood up, and I was about to go when suddenly Tyson grabbed my arm and stopped me.*

*'Listen to me, Ares,' he shouted to me, 'she's my sister, and I know she can handle this. If you go to her now, you will make her weak, and she will depend on you all the time. I know it's very difficult for you to see her like this, but you have to do this for her if you really do love her, Ares. I will guarantee you that she will never hate you or stop loving you. Please try to understand me. This is good for her.'*

*I stared at him and got even angrier.*

*'Why had this to be so damn hard?' I yelled out to Tyson.*

*'I know, but you have to be strong for 'your' Angel. If you break down like this, then imagine what would happen to her. Don't forget, Ares, you're doing this for Angel to give her a better life.' Tyson said calming me down.*

*He was right; I had to be strong for my Angel. I knew it was going to be hard, but it was only for a couple of years, and after that we would be together. Even though it was raining heavily, I could still see tears coming from Tyson's eyes, and I could see that our love was true as it had affected so many people.*

*I had to do one thing which was very important for my Angel and to prove that I really did love her which was to talk to her parents.*

When I opened my eyes, I realised I was back in my university apartment. I wish I could forget all the memories I had of Ares, but the more I tried, the harder it got to forget him. After what he had done to me at my worst time, how come I couldn't forget him? I just couldn't figure it all out. There surely had to be a reason to this.

# Chapter 11

## Ares without Angel

*This was the day I have to do this, not for myself, but for my Angel; I knocked on the door a few times and finally someone opened the door. A lady opened the door and asked me who I was looking for.*

*'Can I see Mr Khan please?'*

*She told me to come in and follow her. When I entered the room, Mr Khan recognised me straight away and stood up. Next to him was a woman who I believe was Mrs Khan as she looked exactly like my Angel; but I knew her personality was completely opposite to that of my Angel's. Now I know where my Angel got her looks from.*

*'Can I help you?' Mr Khan asked me with a deep voice.*

*'I think you know who I am, Uncle. I'm Ares. I came here today just to let you know that I truly do care about Angel. The hardest decision I have made in my life is not to bother my Angel for a couple of years and that is because I want her to finish her college and university without any disruptions. Not only this but also I want to make my life as perfect as I can, so that in the future when I'm with her, I don't ever want her to say I don't have something. That's all I wanted to say, Uncle.' As I finished off, I started walking back towards the door and halfway down the corridor,*

*I stopped, turned around, and in Farsi, I said, 'Please keep my Angel happy always.' When I got to the door, I saw Sonya standing there.*

'Khoda hafiz *(goodbye) future brother-in-law,' she said to me smiling.*

*I smiled back at her. 'Keep your sister happy always,' I said and walked out of the house.*

**Two years later**

*I think my Angel is praying for me, because since I have left university, my work has been fantastic; I have been working in this company for only six months and already they promoted me to be the head manager of the company. It really is a miracle. However, the hardest thing is that I'm without the love of my life. I never knew it was going to be this hard. Everywhere I go, I see my Angel, everything I do, I see my Angel, and every girl I look at, I see her face. It's crazy. For me, the whole world looks like my Angel. I tried to get her out of my head but I couldn't. Even during one of my meetings, I saw her behind the glass windows mouthing something to me. That time it felt so real, like she was actually there. I quickly left the meeting room and when I finally got to the window, I realised it was my imagination again, and that it wasn't real. But at the end of the day, I know this is the only way I can be with my Angel; it's for her own good. However, it got even harder when I bought the house in her name, because I can see her face everywhere in this house. Every room I go to, she's there.*

*It was around 8.00 p.m. when I went to the balcony for fresh air and saw my Angel there; she smiled at me. I smiled to myself and hugged her from behind and she gently put her head on my shoulder. I kissed her on her cheek and tried to see what she was staring at. Then I realised she was staring at the sunset; it was a beautiful scene which I'd never noticed before, and I looked back at my Angel and I saw my arms where empty. I knew it was too good to be true; of course she wouldn't be there. I smiled to myself and went back inside. I sat on the couch and closed my eyes. When I opened them, I saw my Angel again coming towards me with a cake in her hands. It had candles. I realised then that it was my birthday that day and I had completely forgotten about it, because all I had in my head was her. She sat next to me, told me to make a wish first and then blow out the candles. My wish was pretty obvious; to have my Angel back in my life very soon. When I blew out the candles, she disappeared again just like before. I think it's time for me to find my Angel, because each day is getting harder and harder for me without her. I don't think I can take anymore without her. I need her back in my life. However, what I have achieved so far I know is not good enough to have her in my life, when her family are such big people. I don't what anyone to look down at my Angel because of me; especially not her parents. I can do this. For her happiness, I will wait another one or two years, and by then, I'm not only going to be the manager, but I will be the owner of the company.*

# Chapter 12

## New Life: Changed Person

It's been three years since I have seen or spoken to any member of my family. I still have hope that one day they will know it wasn't my fault and they will take me back home. However, I know the chance of that happening is very small. At the end of the day, they are my family; I know they will come for me. I know that some day my family will be behind that brown door. Every time I think about them, I get so emotional and I can't talk about it to anyone either. I know I have Amar and Kiran, but when I talk to them, they get mad at me as I get very emotional. However, I'm very lucky that I always have Allah with me; I have been guided towards the right direction since I left home and that's because I have Allah with me. I wiped my tears away and said to myself, 'Ohh, Allah, all this which has happened in my life is my own fault. I wish I'd listened to them then, and now I wouldn't be here all alone.' I started crying with my head on my study table.

'Angel!' yelled Amar as he walked into my room and stood me up. 'What the hell is wrong with you? Snap out of it! What do you mean if you listened to them? Listen to what? They made your life a living hell and they don't give a damn where or how you are, and you're sitting here crying for them?' he finished off.

'*They are my parents. How dare you talk about them like that!*' I shouted and at the same time pushed him away. 'OK, fine. The way they were to me was unfair. I accept that, but I know they never hated me. They were like that because they loved me so much and they wanted the best for me, especially my mum. But look how I repaid them for their love. By bloody finding a guy and giving them a bad name. You think that's right? Is this how a Muslim girl should be? Like me? Then what's the bloody difference between a Muslim and non-Muslim girl? I get it. For them, it's their culture, but not for us. Come on, tell me, Amar.' I couldn't take it anymore and I just broke down on the floor and continued crying even more. Amar stood me up and wiped my tears.

'I'm sorry, Sis. I didn't mean to say all that to you. I just can't stand it when you blame everything on yourself, knowing it's not your fault. Maybe you think it's your fault, but I don't, and it kills me to see my baby sister being hurt like this. It's my responsibility to keep you happy.' He wiped my tears away again and hugged me. Kiran came with Sam into my room from where they were standing outside and stood next to us. The following morning when I woke up, it felt like I had been sleeping for the past three or four days. It felt so long. I don't know why. I sat on my bed, and when I looked down on the floor, I couldn't believe what I saw. I really couldn't believe that they did this for me. All three of them were sleeping on the floor of my room. Then I realised I was not alone. I had never been alone. They are my family. I had them all along, but I never noticed till then.

'Angel, Angel, where are you?'

I heard Amar calling me from the corridor. I got the feeling he must have panicked when he woke up and saw I wasn't in my bed. I smiled to myself and called out, 'I'm in the kitchen. Don't worry, I'm still alive.'

'Hey! I don't want to hear that kind of stuff from your mouth. Do you understand?' he said as he walked into the kitchen.

'I can't believe you all slept on the floor of that tiny room, and anyway, there was space in the living room as well, now that all the students have gone back home. Why did you all squash yourselves in there?' I asked Amar.

'Because we didn't want to be away from our Angel,' Kiran said, walking in and giving me a hug at the same time.

'I love you, too, babes,' I replied back with a smile.

'Where is Sam?' Amar asked Kiran. When he said that, we both looked at each other and yelled out together, 'Oooowwww!' and we both started laughing.

'What? You two are just jealous that we care about each other so much and you two don't,' Sam said as she came in.

'Of course we care about each other. When you weren't here, I came in and gave Angel a hug, and she told me she loved me. Don't see you two doing that. Shows that you two are jealous of us,' Kiran said, laughing.

'Why would we be jealous of lesbians? Am I right, babe?' Sam said, looking at Amar and then went into his arms.

'Yeah, you're right about Kiran. She is a bit dodgy, but no sister of mine is going to be a lesbian,' Amar said, smiling towards me.

'Hey! Who you calling dodgy? You're dodgy!' Kiran yelled out from the other side of the table.

'Calm down, I'm just joking. Don't kill me,' he replied, still smiling.

'You two will never stop teasing each other. You're both like Tom and Jerry,' I said laughing and Sam joined in. After we had our breakfast, Amar suggested that we should all go out to celebrate. Firstly, because we all passed our second year of university, and secondly, because I never go out, and thirdly, to get late birthday gifts, since on my birthday I was crying like always.

When we went out, we all really had a fantastic time together. Well, I don't know about the rest of them, but I really enjoyed myself, and I think that's because I never go out, so every little thing seemed fun to me. It was around 5.00 p.m., I think. We all got really hungry since we had our breakfast really early, so Amar recommended this really nice, cosy restaurant. The inside was so nice and welcoming. I can't really describe it; but you know those kinds of places that you go in and it feels so pleasant and relaxing. Yeah, I know I'm not making any sense. My point is that it was nice. After we finished eating, Kiran and Sam gave me their gifts, which I wasn't expecting at all, but Amar didn't give me anything at all.

'Give me your hand, Angel.' He took a key out of his pocket and placed it in my hand.

'What is this for?' I looked confused.

'Welcome home,' he replied.

Then I realised that it was the key of the apartment where all three of them live.

'Before you say anything, please listen to us first,' Amar said. He continued, 'Last year, we asked you to live with us. You said no, but this year you have no choice, as we need you just as much as you need us, and it's my responsibility to keep you happy. So please, Angel, don't refuse. Or I will force you.'

I gave him a smile and I didn't even get the chance to think about it as Kiran and Sam both continued begging me since Amar mentioned it. I had no choice but to say yes.

'OK, I will.'

'Yeeeeeeeeeeeees! We going to share a room together! Isn't that great?!' Kiran yelled out, hugging me.

'Hey, you can share a room, but no lesbian stuff towards my sis,' Amar said, laughing.

'I hate you so much, Amar! Stop saying that kind of stuff in public. If someone hears you, they're going to think I'm a lesbian,' she replied back.

The next day, Amar suggested I should move in with them. Since the summer holidays had started, no one was going to be on the campus, and I would be moving anyway. So it didn't make any difference if I moved then or a month later. He was right. Since I was a changed person, I might as well start enjoying my life with the people I could not live without, since they were the only family I had.

A few weeks after I moved in, I wished I had moved in the year before as it was fantastic! It felt like having my family back. I always had someone after me, telling me to eat, not to do this and that (that was usually Amar as he was the boss). And Kiran—she was the joy of the house. Without her, the house would be really strange and very quiet.

That afternoon, it got very hot. Well, as it was August and the hottest month. What else would you expect except sunshine? Amar and Sam went out somewhere, and Kiran was in the shower like always. She had a shower at least three times in one day. I think that's too much.

There was a cafe just outside our house. It was really nice, especially in the summer, as it had glass all around. So I decided to go there for a Frappuccino as it was really hot and I was really tired. I told Kiran I would be there and that after she finished, she could meet me at the cafe. I don't know why, but it felt really weird when I entered the café. I mean, I go there at least three or four times a week, but I don't know why it felt so strange then. I don't know, maybe because I never went there alone. Yeah, I think it was that. I got my chocolate Frappuccino. Well, I love chocolate. I have chocolate with everything. Anyway, as I was drinking my Frappuccino, I noticed a figure standing in front of me. I looked up to see who it was. I couldn't believe my eyes . . . It couldn't be him . . . I never thought I would see him again in my life.

# CHAPTER 13

## Past Comes Back Haunting

No, of course it wasn't him; he just looked like him a lot, that's all. The strangest thing was that he just continued staring at me and finally said, 'I'm sorry. It's just, you're so beautiful, and you look like someone who's very special to me.'

He sounded so familiar and why did my heart beat faster when I heard his voice? No, it couldn't be him. As I stared at him, I understood that it was him. My eyes started to water and I finally managed to say, 'A . . r . . . e . . . s, is that you?' My heart started breaking.

'Angel, my Angel,' he whispered with his eyes full of water just like mine, and he looked down at the ring on my finger. I couldn't stand being there anymore. I had to leave. I stood up and I was about to run out when he called me from behind.

'Please don't go. I can feel how hurt you are, and please don't cry, because it's killing me. I can't stand seeing you hurt like this.' His voice started breaking.

I turned around and I just wanted to shout at him and scream, 'Why the hell do you care now?!' But if I did that, he would think I was still that vulnerable girl who depended on him. I had to be strong and give him an answer like an adult. I wiped my tears away.

'If me being upset for a second kills you, then why did you disappear from my life for the past three years? Who was my replacement? Don't come back in my life now that you lost everything and start lying to me again.'

'What? No no one can take your place. Please just give a chance to explain why I did that,' he replied with a very hurt voice. I sat back down.

'Why have you come back into my life? Is it because you just found out I have found happiness finally and it's killing you? Is that it? Well, guess what, Ares? It's not going to happen this time as I'm not that seventeen-year-old, vulnerable girl who needed a shoulder to cry on. Now, I'm an independent, twenty-year-old woman who can look after herself. So please get out of my life and leave me alone forever. You left me, you hurt me, you broke my heart, you crushed my world, Ares!' Tears rolled down my pink cheeks.

'Angel, please just listen to me for five minutes, and after that, I promise you I will disappear forever from your life,' he begged me.

'Listen to what, Ares? To your lies? To your fake promises? Do you see those three people out there?' I pointed towards the glass window where Amar, Kiran, and Sam were standing. 'When I had no one and was at my worst time, I chose you over them, because I thought after my family, you would be my future. But that was the biggest mistake I made in my life, as I was wrong. You're not my family. They are, because they have been with me every single step of the way since you left me, since my family left me, and since my world became a living hell.' I finished off, crying, and ran out of the cafe to Kiran, Sam, and Amar.

He ran after me. I could hear him behind me, but only his footsteps. I didn't care. I just wanted to get away from him, never see him again in my life, as every time I remembered that day, what he did to me, I just wanted to disappear somewhere that there was no sign of Ares. I continued running and running. I wanted to get somewhere quiet with no one around and stay there. But my heart kept shouting Ares's name. But my mind was telling me to run and never look back.

Finally, I got to this pond with lots of trees around it and a bench near it. It was so quiet and peaceful with no people around it. I sat down on the bench and started talking to God.

'Why, Allah? Why have you sent him back into my life now that I have found happiness? Because of him, I have lost everything, and now I don't want him back,' I continued, crying.

'Angel, please listen to me.'

I heard his voice behind me and I stood up screaming, 'Stay away from me, Ares! If you come near me, I swear by Allah's name I will kill myself! Tell me, h . . . o . . . w, how could you leave me like that? Just the day my parents kick me out of the house, just the day I lose everyone, you walked out from my life, too. Tell me why?'

Behind him, I saw Amar, Kiran, and Sam all coming my way, and I ran towards Amar, crying. Amar hugged me and I said to him, 'Tell him to go away, Amar. Please tell him not to come back and ruin my life again. Please.'

'Look, Angel. Look, calm down. Your brother is here now. I will make everything OK, I promise,' he said, calming me down.

'Someone tell me why Angel is not with her parents!' Ares shouted out like an innocent soul who didn't know anything, which really made me mad.

'Because of you, you idiot! I lost everything! My parents always used to tell me never replace your family with a stranger, as you will lose your family and the stranger will leave you. But I was a stupid child who didn't listen to them, and that's exactly what happened to me. You think after my dad saw me with you he would still allow me to come back to his home? Why do you think I came to you that day? Because I missed you?! No, it was because they kicked me out of their life and their home! I had no place to go. That's why I came to you. But you didn't bother listening to me. You told me to get lost, just like them. However, I was lucky enough to have these three special people in my life that looked after me all this time!' I yelled out at the top of my voice so he could get it in his head.

'What?' he said in shock, like someone stabbed him with a knife. But I didn't care; I just wanted to get away from him. So I looked at Amar, and he understood straight away what I wanted. He called Kiran and Sam over and told them to take me home, but he stayed with Ares. I don't know why.

*'Why did none of you tell me all this?' I demanded from Amar. 'You and Kiran both had my number. Why didn't you bother phoning me? If I knew this was the case, I would have never left her. The only reason I did that was to keep her happy and to give her a perfect future. Why didn't you tell me, damn it?!'*

*'What the hell do you expect me to say after what you did that day?' Amar said, pushing me away. 'That day, I wanted to run after you and kill you, because of your stupidity. She's my sister, damn it, and her happiness means everything to me! So we all tried to keep her happy all these years and we tried to keep your crazy actions away from her mind!' Amar shouted.*

*He was right. He did have a point. It was entirely my fault. I should have listened to Angel. When Amar finished telling me everything, I couldn't believe how much pain my Angel had been through, and all by herself. I didn't blame her for hating me so much. If I was in her place, I would hate myself too. I would make it up to her. I promised this to Angel. But still, it was not too late. If I told Angel the truth: why I did that, then she would forgive me. I turned to Amar.*

*'Listen, you have to find a way for her to talk to me. That's the only way I can prove to her that I did all this because of her, not for myself. Please, Amar,' I begged him.*

*'You're asking for a big favour. But since I know you will keep my sister happy, I'll try,' he replied. 'But don't forget, I'm doing this for my sister's happiness, not for yours. If you hurt her again, I swear to God, I will hunt you down, and I don't care how long it takes me, as she has been through a lot. I don't want any more pain in her life. Do you understand me?' he finished off with a threat.*

*'You're not going to get that opportunity as I will fill every second of her life with love and happiness,' I answered him. He smiled at me, shook my hand, and wished me luck. I wished him the same, and he walked away.*

*With that sorted, I needed to go and see Mr and Mrs Khan. They needed to answer some of my questions which they couldn't answer three years ago.*

*As one of their staff opened the door, I straight away went in, completely ignoring whatever he was saying, as this time there was no room for respect. Before, I did it for my Angel. Since they didn't want her, I had no reason for respecting them. When I walked into the living room, both Mr and Mrs Khan stood up when they saw me. That's not because they respected me, since after three years, they still knew who I was.*

*'Let me guess. You have come for Angel?' Mr Khan said with a very deep voice. I looked down and then up towards him.*

*'No, sir, as I just found out, she wasn't in this house for the past three years. I came here that day. Why didn't you tell me you had kicked her out of your house and you didn't know where she was?' I demanded from Mr Khan.*

*'How dare you talk to me in that manner? Didn't your parents teach you any manners?' Mr Khan raised his voice. 'We know she's been with you all this time. That's why we didn't bother looking for her. If she was from my blood, then she wouldn't have left the house, even if we told her to. The only reason she went was because she was waiting for an opportunity to blame it on us. To us, she's dead. I have no daughter by that name. Do you understand?!' he finished off.*

*I couldn't believe what I was hearing. After all these years, they still thought their daughter who is more pure and cleaner than a real angel would do this to them? It really was shocking, and I thought it was time for me to tell them the truth. But I knew it was too late for them and me to get our Angel back into our lives.*

*'With all due respect, sir, I beg you. Please say whatever you like about me, but not about my Angel who's so pure and clean. You don't know what your daughter has been through all these years, and all by herself with no family.' I began telling them everything Amar told me that my Angel had been through and the times when she was talking to me, the problems she had. When I finished off, Mrs Khan broke down on the living room floor, screaming, 'What have I done! How can I be such a*

*terrible mother to my little girl?!' she continued crying. I stood her up and Mr Khan put his hand on my shoulder.*

*'What do you suggest we do, son? Please help us get our daughter back,' he said with a broken voice. It felt so good when he called me son. That meant he trusted me and knew I hadn't done anything to bring shame to his family's name.*

*'Firstly, Aunty, you need to pull yourself together, as we all now know how much pain Angel has been through at such a young age and all by herself. The last thing she needs in her life is pain. So please, no more crying, Aunty. Just forget the past and give her all the happiness she needs now.'*

*'Well, I can tell she absolutely hates me as when I saw her, she wasn't willing to listen to anything I had to say. She keeps blaming herself for everything that happened in this house, not any of you. Amar told me she always says she has made the biggest mistake of her life by choosing me, as because of me, she has lost her family.' When I finished, tears started coming into my eyes as something inside me kept telling me I might lose my Angel.*

*'I can't believe after what I have put her through she still blames herself and loves us this much. She truly is a Khan,' Mrs Khan said to Mr Khan. I'm glad they are finally coming to their senses.*

*'OK, I have asked Amar to convince Angel to speak to me because I know she will only listen to him, as she sees him as a brother and he is one of the people that she trusts the most. I just want to have the opportunity to tell her that I did all this for her. If I knew that day what had happened, I would have never left her,' I said to them.*

*'Listen, son, I know my daughter. If she trusts someone with all her problems, as much as she hates you, I will guarantee you, she will understand you,' Mr Khan advised me.*

*Let's hope they are right. I told them that I would keep in contact with them after Angel agreed to meet and discussed what to do next.*

'Angel, Angel, where are you? I want to talk to you.'

I could hear Amar calling me as soon as he entered the house. I knew he was going to talk to me about Ares. I didn't want to hear it as I had forgotten about him. If we talked about that idiot again, I would get hurt, which he is not worth. As soon as he entered the living room, I went out, as I couldn't stand him sticking up for that idiot instead of his own sister.

'Angel, please listen to me.'

I completely ignored him and continued walking away from him.

'Please,' he said very calmly and I just had to stop and listen to what he had to say.

'Look, please just go and see him once and you will understand everything. I promise you that.'

'What the hell is wrong with you, Amar? What could Ares possibly say to you that you changed your mind 180 degrees? Have you forgotten that you're the one who hated him more than me, and now you want me to go and see him? No. Seriously. Tell me, Amar, are you feeling OK or have you forgotten the past? Well, if you have, let me remind you that this is the same guy who ruined my life, the same person who took my family away from me. Tell me, Amar, whose side are you on? Me or him? Pick one, not both.'

I walked away, crying. He followed me into my room.

'Angel, look you know how much I love you. All these years, I was searching for a way to keep you happy. If I have to pick, of course I will pick you over him, because at the end of the day, you're my sister and he's nobody to me. I could tell you everything right now, but I'm not going to. I want you to hear it from Ares. That's why I want you to go and see him. Please do this for me. It's the last favour I will ask from you.' He put his hands over my hands.

He left me alone in my room to think about it, and the more I thought, the more I didn't want to see his face, because every time his name came into my head, I remembered what he did to me. However, somehow Amar had seen a different face, and because of my brother, I would see him. But I didn't understand why he came back into my life when I had finally found happiness. Why wasn't he there at my worst time, when I needed him desperately? None of it made sense, and I hoped he'd better have one damn good explanation tomorrow.

The next day as I was getting ready to see him, the same thought I had the night before kept coming back and I still didn't know why I was doing this to myself. This guy was not worth it. I'm not doing this for him anyway. I'm doing it for Amar's sake.

I got ready and Amar told me to meet him by that small pond where this hell scene started. He also mentioned that I should not argue with him and should listen to what he had to say, which would be very hard for me. When we got there, he was already waiting for me. I looked at Amar with anger because he made me do this. Amar kissed me on my forehead, gave me a hug, and whispered in my ear, 'Please, Sis, listen to what he has to say.'

I breathed out deeply and started telling myself I had to do this not only for Amar, but also for myself. I gave him a warm smile indicating that I would, and he drove away.

All of a sudden, I felt something touching me. When I turned to see, it was Ares. Quickly, I moved away from him.

'Look, I promised Amar that I will listen to you. That doesn't mean you have the right to touch me, because you lost that right three years ago, do you understand?' I said very seriously.

'OK, I'm sorry. But can I just say you changed so much. I mean, you're so beautiful and you have grown into this mature woman that it's absolutely breathtaking to look at,' he said smiling at me. Maybe he has changed a bit, but inside he's still the same Ares.

'Well, people do change. They don't stay the same and if that's what you have come to say to me, then I'm leaving or get to your actual point,' I replied with a serious voice.

He began telling me the reasons why he went mad that day, how he didn't know I wasn't living with my parents, that he wanted me to do well in my studies, so he left me because of that and to make my future perfect by going away and working. When he finished, I looked at him like 'what the hell was wrong with him' back that day. I mean, OK, I was grateful that he had worked hard and he had cared about my studies, but for God's sake, I wasn't a kid. He could have told me. He wanted a final answer. Well, I would give him one, but calmly like Amar told me.

I began, 'I appreciate what you have done for me, but do you think that by you making me a millionaire or buying whatever I want, it will make me forget my past? No, Ares. You still don't know the meaning of love. What the hell am I going to do with all these things when I don't have my family, when every second I have to be terrified that you are going to leave me any minute just like before? I'm sorry, Ares, but that's not the life I wanted or planned to have, and you know that. OK, I agree when you say it would have been difficult for me, but I wasn't a five-year-old girl who wouldn't understand what's good for her and what's not. But you know what the worst thing was? You dropped the bomb on my worst day, when I needed you the most.' I finished off and started walking away from him.

'Angel, please listen to me,' he said as he called me from behind. That was it. I couldn't take it anymore. I know I promised Amar I would be calm, but this guy had gone too far.

'No! You listen to me, Ares!' I shouted out as I turned towards him. 'Let me tell you something. I worked far too hard to achieve this life, and I'm not going to let you or anybody else take it away from me. Do you understand? You were lonely without me. Well, I'm really sorry, but you don't know what the hell I have been through the past three years. So don't come here and tell me you need me back because you feel lonely. I'm going to say this in the nicest way I can, so you will understand. Stay away from me!' I walked away with tears coming down my face as I still loved this guy so much that it's beyond description.

I knew my life would be incomplete without him. However, being with him would be like throwing myself in hell, because my Ares had changed. He was not the same guy I met four years ago.

'Didn't I tell you I don't want to see any more tears in your eyes?' I heard a familiar voice. When I looked up, it was Amar. I ran into his arms and continued crying.

‘I told you, Amar, don’t make me go, but you didn’t listen,’ I said, crying.

‘OK, I’m really sorry. Please, Angel, stop crying,’ Amar said calmly, with a very hurt voice. He opened the car door and helped me in. As he stared driving, he continued telling me to calm down and kept repeating himself, as he was sorry for making me go see him.

When we got home, Kiran and Sam came running and started asking me if everything was OK. I didn’t say anything as I wasn’t in the mood to talk about him again. Then Amar gave them a sign indicating that they should leave me be. I went straight to my bedroom and fell asleep, because maybe in my dreams I would finally be in my own perfect world, which I couldn’t achieve in reality.

# Chapter 14

## Ares Needs to Win His Angel Back

*I had to do something. There was no way I was losing my Angel again. OK, maybe she was right. What I did was wrong, but it was not my fault that I didn't know her parents did that to her. I blamed all this on her parents. If they had stopped judging her so much and kept her happy, I would have never lost her. However, that was the past. At that time, I had to win her back. I would do anything to have her back. The only person that could help me with this was Amar.*

*'Hello, hello, Amar. It's Ares,' I said on the phone, but the only thing I could hear was people talking and no answer. Maybe he's with Angel and trying to calm her down. I'll wait for a couple of minutes. He might talk.*

*'Hello, what is it? Why are you phoning me again? You asked me for a favour and I did it, but now I wished I didn't, because I don't know what the hell you have said to her that she's this hurt. I don't want to do anything else for you!' he shouted and put the phone down. Man, what was I supposed to do?*

*I phoned him again. 'Look, please listen to me, Amar. Just for a minute.'*

*'Fine, what do you want?' he answered back in a bad mood.*

*'I know she's very hurt, however, the only reason is because she still loves me. I can see it in her eyes. Trust me, Amar.'*

*'Yeah, right,' he said interrupting me.*

*'Trust me. I could see it in her eyes. Why do you think she's so hurt? You think it's because she saw me? Nah, your wrong, Amar. It's because she still has feelings for me and she thinks I'm a bad person. Therefore, she cannot be with me. Do you understand what I'm trying to say?'*

*He went completely silent for a couple of minutes and finally answered back.*

*'I think you make sense, but I really don't want to help you. However, I don't have any choice. I have to do it for my sister's happiness, but this doesn't mean we are friends.'*

*'OK,' I said laughing. This guy was funny, but who cares as long as he helped me. 'I think the only way she will forgive me is for me to unite her with her family as when I saw her, she kept saying I took her family away from her,' I said to Amar.*

*'Have you forgotten that they hate you more than Angel? So what makes you think they will listen to you?' he questioned me.*

*'Don't worry about that. I have already spoken to them. They love their daughter and me even more,' I replied with a huge smile on my face.*

*'OK, fine. If you want her back, then this time you have to do it my way or I'm out,' he told me.*

*'OK, that's fine. Whatever you say, I'll do that,' I replied. He was right, because we tried my way and it didn't work.*

*'I know it's going to be hard for you, but if you want her back, then you have to do this, Ares. In a month's time, her university classes will start again, and she needs to concentrate on her studies. So you need to wait till May next year until she finishes university. I know it sounds long, but if you don't, I will guarantee you that she will drop out of university because of you, and I'm sure you don't want that. So just go back to you work, you can phone us regularly to check how she is, and by then, we all will try to convince her that you're a good person.'*

*He was completely right, but another year sounded so long. However, it was better to wait a year than all eternity.*

*When I put the phone down, I felt so alone because I really thought I would have my Angel back. I never thought I would have to wait this long, but she's worth it.*

*The next day, I phoned Mr Khan and explained the situation to him. He disagreed with Amar's decision and told me that if they were there for her now, then she would be able to concentrate with her studies. She loved her parents and wanted them back. I knew Angel was waiting for the day her parents would walk through the door of her life again. I, too, agreed with Mr Khan, so we decided to come up with a plan to win Angel's heart back and to un-break her heart.*

# Chapter 15

## Grief, the Price We Pay for Love

Summer started to end, and the nights became longer as the days became shorter. But that day, it was different. Everything looked and felt different. The weather. The atmosphere. Everything. I even got up in a happier mood. My mind started to question my happy mood, my heart started to feel the happy mood, and my blood got warmer. I knew that today something extraordinary was going to take place, so I just had to get up and face the day. I got up from my bed and headed towards the bathroom, but the vibration of my phone stopped me as a text message came through:

Amar*: Angel wake up and make sure the house is clean.*

Once again, my feelings and thoughts were right. I rushed to the bathroom and took my morning shower and got ready as fast as I could. Then I raced around my little room and cleaned the whole place up. Finally, I was free to ring Amar. I sat on my breakfast table and the call went through to Amar. He picked up really quickly.

'Amar, what's going on? I got your message.'

'So how come you're ringing me two hours later?' he laughed.

'Oh, I'm sorry. I was tidying my room up, and I had a shower. Why, what's going on?'

'Oh, it's nothing bad, Angel, just that . . . well, guess what . . . ?' he paused for a minute. Then he continued. 'Mum and Dad are coming to visit you today!' he exclaimed on the phone.

'Come on, Amar, I'm not in a mood for your jokes and it's not funny,' I said very annoyed.

'I swear I'm not joking. Trust me, Angel,' he said.

'Oh my god, Amar! Are you serious? All those years of waiting, all those months of dreaming for them to walk through this door has finally come. They finally did. Today is the day!'

'Yes, sis, once again you win. Good won, again. See you later. Call me when they arrive and I will be there too.'

'Amar,' I paused. 'But how did they contact you?' I asked him.

He replied, 'You need to thank Ares for that.'

'OK,' I replied. 'Please take care, and come home soon. I love you'

'Yes, I will, Angel. Don't worry. I love you, too.' Then the phone hung silent.

I got ready and just waited and waited. Every second felt like a century, the clock kept ticking, and the handle felt as if it was moving slower and slower. I stared at the door. All those days and months that I went through, alone, thinking and thinking that one day, just one day, my parents would walk through that door, take my hand, and go home with me. And that day finally had arrived.

Suddenly, the door bell rang.

'Du-du-du' my heart kept beating. I could feel my whole body sweating; my blood was boiling hot, just like a kettle that had finished boiling water. The whole world stood still for a split second. Then I forced myself to open the door. There they were. My parents stood right in front of me. Mum was wearing a black sweater and white trousers, while Dad had his suit on; must have finished from work, I figured. A sudden voice echoed through my head, 'Get out of my house, Angel. You're not from my blood anymore.'

Then tears flowed from my eyes. It was like a sea had calmed down, the waves were warmer than ever. My whole body shut down, and I froze into one piece.

'Angel, are you OK?' my dad asked frightfully.

I pulled away and sat on the floor. But my eyes were still looking at my dad's eyes.

Suddenly . . . when tears flowed from my dad's eyes, I snapped back to reality and hugged him as tight as I could.

'Dad, please, I had given you too many of these, I can't bear to see tears again in your eyes.' They both came up to me and helped me from the floor and hugged me tight, close to their hearts.

'Forgive us,' mum cried.

'Forgive me,' I cried.

Minutes later, we walked to the kitchen table and had a cup of tea. While they were drinking their tea, I called Amar.

'Hello!' I exclaimed.

'Hello,' an unfamiliar voice came through.

'Excuse me, but could you give the phone to Amar, please?' my voice started to shake.

'I'm sorry, miss, but unfortunately, we can't.'

'What do you mean you can't? Give the phone to him now!' I screamed.

'Please, Ms Angel, calm down. We are on our way to your flat now.' The phone hung silent.

I stood there as the scene blacked out. My hand started to shake, and the phone fell out of my hand.

'Angel, you OK?' Dad shook me.

'Angel, Angel, Angel,' my mum echoed silently.

Then, minutes later, I came back to my right state of mind. I managed to get myself up and sat on the chair. I sat staring at the white wall around the kitchen. I noticed a pattern on the wall which I had never seen before, and I figured I was concentrating too hard, thus the patterns were just appearing. What was wrong with me? I had no idea. I knew the news concerning Amar was not good. My stomach kept knotting. The knots got tighter. And tighter. I felt my stomach twisting and turning. Then, slowly, drop by drop, tears rolled down my cheeks.

There was a knock at the door . . . it made me jump. Mum and Dad sat on the sofa, while I got up and went towards the door with my sweaty palm, I turned the doorknob and opened the door.

'Hello, I'm Officer Morris and we need to take you to the hospital,' the police officer explained.

'W-h-a-t for?' I spoke forcefully.

'I would rather you come with us first, and we explain to you on the . . . '

Before he could finish his sentence, I grabbed my coat and walked out. The police officers followed, and I heard one telling my parents to come to the hospital. My mind kept questioning me, *Why is he there? What has happened to him?* . . . Rapidly, question after question kept going round in my mind. My body felt tense. My blood got warmer. Then my mind just blacked out.

One hour later, the police car parked by the door of Central Hospital. I realised that we were parked outside Accident and Emergency. Then I was sure that what I was thinking was right; something terrible had happened. I was sure of that then. My body was shaking, I was sweating more and more, and my heart started to pump faster and faster. I walked through the automatic door. It felt like walking straight into death. The scene was like a quick snapshot of a horror movie; it was still, silent . . . everything had been blacked out—everywhere but one room . . . Room 786. I walked past the silent-horror-movie scene straight up to that room.

The light bulb was flicking and irritating my left eye. I pulled the white sheet off, and I could not believe my eyes . . . my heart could barely beat. My head started to spin. My palms started to sweat and as for my body . . . it started to shake more and more. 'A . . . m . . . a . . . r,' my voice broke. I could barely take each letter out of my mouth. My tongue started to knot, and my stomach started to knot even harder.

'A m a r . . . is that you? Amar, open your eyes, *Jaan*. I am here. Look, it's Angel, your sister. Amar, please open your eyes. A . . . m . . . a . . . r?' I took his cold, pale, purple hand. His fingers were so cold, and they had no sign of life in it.

'Amaaaaaaaaaaar!' I shouted at the top of my voice. 'Amar, please wake up. I'm here. Someone please tell him to open his eyes!' I kept screaming at the top of my voice. The doctors came rushing into the ward.

'Take her away,' the doctor demanded of one of the nurses.

'Get off me! I'm not going anywhere without Amar. Let me go!'

Ares pulled me out of the ward.

'Get off me, this is your fault, Ares! I hate you! Why did you come into my life? When you weren't in my life, Amar was alive. He was with me! Why? Tell me why?' I grabbed his collar and shouted at the top of my voice. Faintly, from the distance, I saw Kiran and Sam. I ran into their arms and we all burst into tears.

'He's gone, and he's not coming back. God needed an angel, and he took him away from us,' I said, with my tears rolling down my cheeks.

'No, Angel! Please tell me you're lying!' Sam screamed.

She started to hit herself, and then Kiran grabbed her and slapped her as hard as she could.

'Stop this madness, Sam! He's gone! He's gone!' Kiran shouted at Sam.

Ares held me tight in his arms. I put my head on his shoulder and started to cry my heart out. Mum and Dad came from a distance and held me in their arms. I dropped to the ground, and my mind just blacked out. Faintly, I saw Kiran's hand on my shoulder. Then, all of a sudden, everything was white.

From a distance, I saw Amar waving, and I ran up to him. We were by our old school.

'Amar?' I stared at him.

'Yeah, it's me, sis.'

'But I thou . . . '

'Yeah, I'm gone. But I guess you were a real angel. You get the chance to say bye to me.'

'Amar, why are you leaving me? I need you, Amar. Please come back,' I cried to him.

'Angel, listen to me,' he hugged me. 'Ares is a very nice boy. He has good intentions and he will keep you happy. Please do this for me and accept him back into your life. Oh, I gave something to the officers to give you, Angel. Be happy always. I love you, sis.' He blew me a kiss.

I didn't even get a chance to say bye.

'Angel, Angel,' my mum's voice echoed.

'Yeah, mum?'

'You OK, sweetie?' she asked.

'Yeah, I think so,' I said as I got up from my bed. Beside me were Kiran, Sam, Ares, and Dad. I knew then I had fainted, but I also knew seeing Amar was real. All my loved ones were beside me. I hugged my girls and Ares kissed my forehead—just like the good old days.

Five days later, it was Amar's funeral. As everyone gathered to say goodbye to him, for every sorry I heard from a relative or a loved one, another tear dropped down my cheeks. As the funeral took place and everyone was saying goodbye to Amar before they buried him, I had a couple of last words to say. As everyone was gathered around me, I started off,

'Amar Yusufi', a brother, a best friend, and the love of someone's life. You brought so much happiness into everyone's life that we all don't know what to do without you. Amar, you showed me the meaning of family. You showed me how it feels to be loved by a family member. You gave me the true meaning of what family means. I am forever grateful, and I know it's better on the other side, and when one day we meet again on the other side, you better be there to hold my hand. Amar, my best friend, my brother, and my smile, you're gone but never forgotten. I will love you forever. I will always love you, *Jaan.*' I finally managed to get the words out. I dropped to the floor and blew a kiss towards him. Ares hugged me and the sun faded away . . .

One thing I learned from my life story is that no matter what's your religion or what you believe in, God will always point you to the right direction. And yes, you will suffer, see and feel a lot of pain but at the end it's worth it all. You will get 100 times more happiness than you expected as long as you believe in God and be patient he will show you the way. Don't forget the more you suffer the more happiness you gain from God, as he's testing you because he wants to see if you can handle the pain, then you definitely can handle the happiness. Never give up as at the end of every pain there is happiness: through every dark tunnel there is a light in the end. You can reach it . . . I did. Some people when they get all the happiness they desire, they take advantage of it and use it in wrong ways as they achieved it so easily. However, if they achieved it in the hard way, they will never choose the wrong directions as they know how much they've been through to get this happiness. You can see for yourself from my experience; so never give up and always have hope.

The End

*Advice for parents*

- Generations have changed and the way you have been brought up is very different from the way you should bring up your child. Therefore, the only way we can get through to them or understand what their problems are is by talking and listening to them.

- Most of the time when they tell us something, we think they are wrong and what we tell them is right. However, that's where most parents make a mistake, because we are all human beings and we are not right all the time. Listen to them and try to understand them in their point of view, as whatever age they are, I'm sure you have been that age too. If they are wrong, then explain to them and tell them where their mistake is and *don't* try to make them do what you want, because they might agree at first, but they will never stick to it. We guarantee this from our own experience, as we have quite strict parents and we love them unconditionally.

- Do not ever be so strict with them that they rebel against you. Give them some freedom. We do understand every culture and religion is different. We mean that you should give them the freedom within your society. However, if you live in a country which is completely different to your culture, then you must adapt to that. By adapting, we mean that the way you were with your kids back home, you have to change that. We both came from a Muslim background, and for us to live the way our parents wanted was very difficult. We went through a lot of disagreements and problems. So from our own experience, we advise other parents not to do that, as not every kid will listen or agree with the strict religion that their parents teach them. Giving your child a tiny bit of freedom will save his/her life and yours.

- During arguments, make sure that when your child is shouting at you, do not say harsh words that will make them angrier. Just try to make them understand why you got angry in the first place.

- Teach them about you culture and the way you want them to have an understanding of their heritage.

- It doesn't matter what is our age; our parents will also be our parents so therefore we crave for their attention. No friend can replace our parents or our family so spend as much time as you can with them. I (Farishta) personally believe that the only time a child would go against their family when that family bond is broken. What I mean by that is; there is no more love and they start looking elsewhere to be loved and to have someone in their life that cares about them.

*Advice for young adults*

- Have respect for your parents no matter what the circumstances are, because at the end of the day, if it wasn't for them, you wouldn't be in this world. The harsher your parents are towards you, the more they love you. We know this, since if it wasn't for the harshness of our parents, we wouldn't have written this book today.

- We know harsh words do hurt a lot, especially when you hear them from your loved ones (i.e. parents, brothers, sisters, or relatives). However, take it in and prove them wrong. What we mean by wrong is, for example if they say 'You're worth nothing,' prove them wrong by doing well for yourself and show them that you are worth everything. We will guarantee you that one day when they realise they are wrong, they will apologise to you. We know this again as we have heard the most harshest words you could imagine from our parents, but we were not hurt by it anymore as we realised that those words have made us very strong people . . . the people we are today.

- Don't ever hide your problems from your parents as we can tell you that parents are the cleverest people in the world. Whether you like it or not, they will find out the truth. Like our mother used to and still tells us, 'I love my kids just like my pupils, as through them I get to see the world, but I keep an eye on them like my enemies.' Her point using the word 'enemy' is that you always closely watch what your enemy does next, so she means that's how close she watches her kids, so that they don't make any mistakes that they would regret later in life.

- Have an understanding of the fact that they were brought up differently, so some views may differ.

- Try to make them understand where your point is coming from and listen to them.

- While arguing, keep your mouth shut so that your parents don't get angrier while they are trying to shout at you. They are your parents and they have the right to shout at you. However, you don't have that right. If you do this, it would be for your advantage, as if they are wrong then they will realise it. We are not saying they will apologise to you. What we are saying is that they have their own way of saying sorry. For example, when our father realised that it wasn't our fault, he used to and still does become extra nice and we straight away knew that he had noticed it wasn't our fault.

- Listen to your parents because they know what's best for you and their aim is always to keep you happy, so yours should be the same. Don't ever think they dislike you, because if that was correct then they wouldn't have brought you into this world. Bringing up a child is not an easy thing.

- We believe that if you keep your parents unhappy, you will never be happy in your life, and whatever you did to your parents, you will get that from your own kids one day. So make sure you always keep them happy.

Lightning Source UK Ltd.
Milton Keynes UK
03 November 2010

162333UK00001B/206/P

9 781453 558362